A Reluctant Dragon

A RELUCTANT DRAGON

A Regency Gaslamp Fantasy

E.B. WHEELER

Rowan Ridge
Press

ISBN 978-1-960033-18-5

First printing: February 2025

Published by Rowan Ridge Press, Utah

Cover and interior design © Rowan Ridge Press

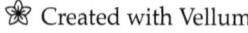 Created with Vellum

Chapter One

A MUD BALL splatted against Arabelle Reynolds' shop window. The glass rattled under the assault, and the mud slurped down the pane, leaving a dirty trail like a slug.

Arabelle froze, needle clenched in her fingers, and watched the mud's progress. Several more blobs followed. Something hot and sick bubbled in her stomach. Why couldn't the anti-magic ruffians leave her alone? She strode to the window, the flare of her fire magic itching to leap free, but she stopped herself and settled for glaring out the window.

All the other ladies in the dress shop—clients and assistants—stopped their chattering and measuring to stare at the spectacle. Arabelle tensed and waited. Waited for them to flood out her door—the back door, of course, to avoid the mud-hurler. Her clients had almost forgotten the anti-magic Luddites attacking her shop previously, and her excellent workmanship drew the ladies of the *beau monde* back despite the scandal. If the attacks started up again, though, all of her hard work would be lost.

"The French!" one of the ladies cried. "It must be."

"What beasts!"

"Our Duke of Wellington and his dragon will put Napoleon in his place."

The general babble of the shop continued along that tenor.

Arabelle sighed and loosened her cramped grip on the needle. She motioned for one of her shop girls to quietly clean the window, then went to help a young lady being fitted for a sprigged muslin gown behind a dressing screen.

Most days, Arabelle ignored the gossip that flowed through her shop like fog rolling off the Thames. Rumors of the Prince Regent's latest tomfoolery or which dragon-linked lady's magic had most impressed the queen did not distract Arabelle from making the finest gowns in London. Her only interest in Napoleon should have been the certainty that military details on gowns would be popular in the upcoming Season. But she'd slept better when Napoleon was imprisoned on Elba and his anti-magic empire dismantled. Since his escape, every piece of news was like a needle prick in Arabelle's back.

"He's gathering a force of anti-magic allies," her young client proclaimed while Arabelle marked out the spot on her gown for some extra ribbon. "There's to be war again."

Arabelle's cat-sized dragon Ruby hopped onto the sill to examine the freshly cleaned shop window. The sun highlighted the red sheen in his brown scales. Napoleon's return to power would stir up all the factions who hated people bonded to dragons and able to do magic. The mud was not the first assault on her shop, but it was the most brazen, occurring in broad daylight. Arabelle didn't even use her fire magic for much beyond heating the water for tea, but that had not stopped the Luddites in the past. The angry mob's shouts echoed in her memory, and she flinched from the figures passing outside her window.

Maria, her head assistant, quickly took up the work Arabelle neglected in her distraction. The girl was competent. No, not girl: young woman. But Maria had worked for Arabelle for eight years. If she was a young woman now, then Arabelle was what?

Not a *young* woman anymore. A spinster, on the shelf, well into her thirties. Old enough that no one questioned it when she began referring to herself by the more dignified "Mrs. Reynolds" instead of "Miss." But only her successful business and her dragon gave her any respectability in London.

A flash of red hair and a solid, masculine figure outside the window caught her eye. Farris—one of Lord Blackerby's Bow Street Runners. She knew Lord Blackerby, as Home Secretary, tasked Farris to keep an eye on her shop, though the anti-magic factions had been quiet since the Battle of the Tower and the death of their leader Shaw almost two years earlier. She doubted Farris's presence was a coincidence after the vandalism of her shop. Some thought that Lord Blackerby would mellow after his marriage to Lady Amelia Chase, but if anything, he was more watchful than ever.

Arabelle could leave Maria to finish the work and chase down Farris to demand news and reassurance. Maria was competent, but this was Arabelle's shop. It was all she had.

She threw herself back into her work, taking up some pins to mark the other side of the dress, making certain every detail would be perfect. The fashion writers at *La Belle Assemblée* had taken note of her designs. A colored image of one of her dresses with favorable commentary in the magazine would seal her success—and unfavorable commentary would destroy her, especially after the fiasco with the mob before and the mud attack today. She could not afford to be less than perfect.

She and Maria finished their task while their young client babbled on about balls and beaus.

Arabelle gave the girl an indulgent smile as she helped her remove the half-finished gown.

Once, Arabelle had also dreamed of dancing in the arms of a handsome man who saw nothing in the world but her. But London had disabused her of any romantic notions. The men in Society were attracted to her dragon magic, but they balanced it against her family's background in trade. None looked past those two factors to see Arabelle herself.

If no handsome lord was coming to whisk her away to a romantic ending, then Arabella would be her own protector, turn her back on Society, and do what made her happy. And she was happy. She looked down at the empty gown in her hands. Most days.

Maria took the gown from her to begin stitching the ribbon, leaving Arabelle to stare at her dragon and worry about Napoleon. No, that would not do. She grabbed her sketchbook and drew a pelisse with a row of military-style buttons that would look charming on a lady while acknowledging England's brave soldiers. After all, they kept the world safe from the forces on the continent that would see magic and dragons wiped out as symbols of a more primitive age.

Arabelle's pencil slowed as she remembered standing on the ramparts of the Tower of London as two great dragons battled for Britain's future. The terror and excitement of it hummed in her chest once again. She shook her head at her foolishness. She and Ruby hadn't even been able to participate lest the chaos dragon replicate her fire magic. It only proved that her shop was where she belonged.

She glanced at Maria. "Is Lady Yates's dress ready for her daughter? She'll expect it by tomorrow."

"Yes, Mrs. Reynolds," Maria said, looking up from her stitching and noticing the sketches. "Oh, were you thinking of adding something like that to the gown? It would look very well."

Arabelle looked between the gown and her sketching. No wonder she had been drawing such silly things! Her subconscious had been trying to improve the dress, which she had not felt was quite perfect.

"Yes, if the gown is otherwise ready, I think we can add a few embellishments. Lady Yates appreciates being at the front of fashion. And it's not worth doing—"

"If we can't do it best," Maria finished Arabelle's favorite phrase for her, flashing a grin.

"Quite right!" That was why *La Belle Assemblée* would soon crown her shop the finest in London.

The bell over her shop door rang. Arabelle put her sketchbook aside and stood to greet the next lady she would adorn.

But it was a man who stood in her doorway—a giant of a man with his hat in his hands and red hair a little disordered. Mr. Farris, the creature of Lord Blackerby.

Chapter Two

ARABELLE QUICKLY EVALUATED Mr. Farris of the Bow Street Runners. Her gaze traveled over his boots—well-polished—past his neat but unassuming trousers and shirt—the waistcoat very tasteful with its simple pattern, the coat tailored to show off a figure muscular from a life of work—and to the cravat, tied expertly but not foppishly.

Maria looked baffled as to what to do with a gentleman in their dress shop. Arabelle felt a strange surge of reassurance at his solid presence, mingled with disquiet at the reminder of her small misadventures on the outskirts of Lord Blackerby's schemes.

She rose and put on a stern expression to hide any nervousness at what news he might bring. Maria mumbled an excuse, gathered her sewing, and fled the room. No one wanted more to do with Lord Blackerby than duty or courtesy required.

Farris cleared his throat. "Good evening, Mrs. Reynolds."

He fidgeted with his hat. His accent bore hints of Scotland. "I'm Mr. Farris—"

"I remember you, Mr. Farris." After all, when the Home Secretary or any of his Runners darkened one's door, it was certain to disrupt one's day. "Have you apprehended the villains who vandalized my shop earlier?"

He crumpled the brim of his hat. "I'm afraid not. We are searching. But Lord Blackerby has many irons in the fire, so to speak."

Arabelle's heart sank. What was she supposed to do against French ruffians if the Bow Street Runners were too busy to help her? "Then unless Lord Blackerby sent you to fetch something for his wife, I can't imagine what business brings you here."

Farris looked taken back by that. Perhaps even slightly hurt? Arabelle might have been a touch too harsh.

She tried to soften her voice, which she knew could be forceful at times. "I shouldn't assume you have no interests outside of Lord Blackerby's service. You have a lady of your own who needs something for her dress?"

Farris's face flushed a red to rival his flaming hair. "N-no! Not at all. That is… That is not to say I don't care for ladies. I just… I don't…" He swallowed and looked down as if her floor had become quite fascinating.

Arabelle wondered what had Farris so tongue-tied. His task must be especially onerous. "You did come on Lord Blackerby's behalf."

Farris looked relieved, and the color slowly settled from his face. "I did. It's not that he doesn't think you worth a personal visit, but he didn't think you would appreciate the attention it would bring."

Farris was correct about that. Everywhere Lord Blackerby

went, his shadows followed, and so did the gossip. The only gossip Arabelle wanted about her shop was related to her stunning designs.

"I suppose I cannot ignore the Home Secretary." She motioned to one of the cushioned armchairs usually reserved for rich mammas hoping to array their daughters in London's finest for their come-outs.

Farris sat carefully, as though afraid he would dirty the cushion. In truth, he was quite respectable looking, if a bit oversized for the delicate chair.

Ruby roused and lifted his head, studying Farris before deigning to approach and roam about the visitor's boots. Farris took this in stride—he worked with the dragon-linked frequently.

Farris looked around the shop, his thoughts seemingly elsewhere.

"Well?" Arabelle prompted. "If you come on Lord Blackerby's behalf, I imagine it has something to do with the rumors I've heard about Napoleon."

Farris gave a guilty start. "Ah, yes. Or rather, only indirectly."

"But it's true that Napoleon has regained his armies?" Arabelle asked.

"Unfortunately, yes. But Lord Blackerby wished for me to call on you because there are few of the dragon-linked attuned to fire."

"For which we should probably all be grateful," Arabelle said.

She knew too well how destructive her ability could be. Fire had no place in a shop full of fine fabric. Once, in her first years as a dressmaker, she had lost her temper trying to set a sleeve and singed the expensive gown.

"Every attunement is important," Farris said. "You're a skilled dressmaker, but you're more than that, too."

Arabelle frowned. If she were a man, they no doubt would welcome her magic. But it was rare that a woman needed such a powerful ability. When she had instinctively used it to defend herself and her shop against the Luddite mob, she had nearly ruined her reputation and her business. *Ackermann*'s magazine had been a breath away from writing a commentary in praise of her work, and now they would not even speak to her.

"And what does Lord Blackerby want with my fire magic?" Arabelle pressed.

"He hopes you're interested in working with him and the other dragon-linked. You could rejoin Society—"

Arabelle huffed. The Home Secretary was quick to ask for help, yet he wasn't offering her any protections—not against ruffians, and not against the possible consequences for her shop. "I am not interested in Society or in people who only come calling because of my dragon or my fire magic. You can tell that to your master—and let him do his own dirty work next time." Arabelle stood. "I believe we are finished here."

Farris worked his mouth a couple of times but seemed to see the futility of arguing with her. He stood as well. "Thank you for your time, then."

As soon as he was out the door, Maria poked her head back into the room, hunting for gossip.

"They want to keep their thumb on me," Arabelle said.

"Would it be so bad to be part of Society?" Maria asked wistfully.

Of course, to the young lady, it probably seemed lovely. Arabelle and Maria spent all their time making dresses for the *beau monde*, and Maria might daydream about wearing them to parties and balls. Being dragon-linked was one of the quickest and surest ways to raise yourself to the height of Society. But that didn't mean Society welcomed newcomers, or that they belonged there.

"I was part of Society for a Season," Arabelle said. "It's wonderful if you enjoy haughty gentlemen evaluating your worth every time you speak to them."

And finding you lacking.

"Or having one fall in love with you," the girl half-mumbled.

None of the gentlemen Arabelle had met seemed interested in love. They'd all been calculating her value. She valued herself enough not to put herself up for sale. Better to run her own business than to become nothing more than an asset to a cold-hearted husband.

As for romance... She was certain some did find it. Perhaps someday she would meet a decent man who appreciated a talented businesswoman. But before she even thought of love, she had to secure her success. Those colored plates in *La Belle Assemblée* would do the trick. She hoped.

Her chest tightened, but she put on a smile and patted her assistant's arm. "I've seen that young man who's courting you. I think you will find love." And with someone who saw her as a person instead of a collection of assets. "In the meantime, we have much sewing to do."

After all, she doubted she'd heard the last from Lord Blackerby or the French.

Chapter Three

FARRIS HATED reporting bad news to Blackerby, and he had bungled that interaction with Mrs. Reynolds. There was something in her dark eyes that bewitched him, as if her magic were over Farris instead of fire. In the interest of duty, he ought to tell Blackerby to find someone else to keep watch over the fascinating dressmaker, but Farris could not bring himself to give up the most beguiling part of his employment.

Blackerby was on edge, though, and this exchange was not going to be any more successful than the one with Mrs. Reynolds—if Farris failed to charm Mrs. Reynolds, he certainly wouldn't charm the intractable earl.

He found his way to Blackerby's office and tapped lightly on the door.

"Come," Blackerby said curtly.

The shadows swirled about the room in agitation, darkening the faint light from the oil lamp. Blackerby, in contrast, sat perfectly still, his boots propped on his table and his eyes fixed on the window, probably seeking secrets from afar.

"Bad news from France?" Farris ventured.

"Bad news from everywhere." Blackerby kicked his feet off the table and swung around. "Napoleon is gathering his forces in France, the Americans are still a thorn in our side, and my man Croft has vanished in Wales."

Farris winced at that. He'd known Croft. He was a good man.

Blackerby's eyes cut to Farris, and he blew out a slow breath. "Tell me you have recruited Mrs. Reynolds."

"She was...resistant, my lord."

Blackerby sighed and rubbed his forehead. Then he chuckled. "Of course she was. She is attuned to fire. It is not easily corralled or controlled."

"She's also an intelligent lady who has a business and a reputation to think of," Farris said before he could think better of it.

Blackerby turned that keen gaze on Farris, studying him speculatively. "Perhaps I should speak with her myself." He grinned. "Few can resist my charms."

Farris smirked in return. "She'll throw you out on your ear."

"What do you suggest? We need someone attuned to fire."

Farris frowned. There it was. Arabelle Reynolds was right that Blackerby was only interested in her for her magic. For what she could do for him. But that was how Blackerby saw everyone. Almost everyone. Farris did not think Lady Amelia Blackerby was a means to an end.

Farris smiled at Blackerby. "You'll never convince Mrs. Reynolds the way you talk. She'll only dig her heels in deeper. You need someone who can connect with her."

"And you think you're the man for the job?"

The tips of Farris's ears warmed at that. Curse his fair Scottish skin. "No, my lord. I think you ought to send your wife. Or Lady Westing. Someone whom Mrs. Reynolds might listen to."

"Ah." Blackerby steepled his fingers. "Yes, it's a delicate situation. Perhaps this is a job for a lady." He cast another speculative glance at Farris. "You're certain you don't wish to try again?"

Farris would love the opportunity to show Arabelle that he didn't see her as a means to an end. That he saw value beyond her dragon and her magic. But there was too much at stake to satisfy his selfish interests.

He shook his head. "No, my lord. Send the ladies into the breach."

Chapter Four

EACH TIME the shop bell rang to announce a visitor, Arabelle tensed. She had defied Lord Blackerby—challenged him—and he would not let that stand. But what could he do? Shove her into a ballgown and drag her by the hair into the ranks of the *beau monde*?

Ha, no, fire would defeat shadow in a direct conflict. Her magic was unpolished, but she could use it, and Lord Blackerby knew it. That was the only reason he or Mr. Farris or any of the others paid her any heed. It would be interesting to know what they had in mind for her and her magic.

She silenced that thought immediately. Society didn't need her. Her shop needed her.

The bell rang again, though dusk gathered in the street—almost closing time. The sound rolled through the shop more like a death knell than a welcome.

Arabelle braced herself and looked up from her stitching.

Instead of Lord Blackerby, it was Lady Phoebe Westing who came through the door—*attuned to light, sparkling eyes, looked best in yellow*—accompanied by Mrs. Eliza Parry —*attuned to water, rich brown skin best accentuated with bold colors*. Their dragons rode on their shoulders.

Arabelle put her work aside and hurried forward to greet them.

"Mrs. Reynolds!" Phoebe exclaimed. "You will not be glad to see us, I'm afraid."

"I'm always happy to see you ladies."

And she was. Not only because they were excellent clients who always paid their bills promptly, but because they spoke to her like a confederate instead of a servant or a castoff. Their dragon magic had opened the doors of Society to them, and unlike Arabelle, they had successfully stepped through. Phoebe had even adopted Arabelle's poor tom cat when the creature had been injured in the mob attack. When *Arabelle* had injured him with her magic. She had not even tried to reclaim the cat, though Ruby missed the company. Arabelle did not deserve a pet if she could not keep it safe.

"We need new traveling gowns, and in something of a hurry," Phoebe said. "I never had a new one made after the baby, and now Eliza—"

"Of course." Arabelle saw it in an instant: Mrs. Parry was expecting.

Eliza smiled. "Yes, I'm certain you see why my old gown won't do. I had almost wondered if it wasn't going to happen for us, but I suppose it's never too late. Not that we will complain about an excuse for some pretty new thing to wear, will we, Phoebe?" Eliza added with a twinkle.

"Though the clothing needs to be practical," Phoebe said with a warning look at Eliza. "The roads in Wales, I've heard, are not always well-maintained."

"Oh, Wales?" Arabelle asked as she beckoned Eliza over and began taking measurements.

It was an odd place to travel, but with war brewing on the continent once again, options were more limited.

"Well, yes." Phoebe shifted and met Eliza's gaze, sharing something in that look. "You see, that's the reason you won't be happy to see us."

Arabelle wrinkled her forehead. Why on earth would their destination matter to her? Or, was it what they were doing in Wales that was the concern? It wasn't likely they had turned spies or any such nonsense. Phoebe's husband was a lord, after all, and they were known to be friendly with...

"Lord Blackerby," Arabelle said, almost a curse.

"He didn't think you would speak with him."

"But I can't throw clients out of my shop," Arabelle almost growled.

A few jittery lights sparkled over Phoebe's head. "You will still have our business regardless of what you decide, but at least hear what we have to say."

Arabelle sighed. "You have until I'm done with these measurements."

"It's the dragon. The fire dragon," Phoebe said quickly. "In Wales."

Arabelle paused, measuring tape stretched across Eliza's shoulders. "What?"

Eliza gave Phoebe a teasing smile. "What Phoebe means to say is that Lord Blackerby needs help with the Red Dragon of Wales. He believes it's a fire dragon, and only someone attuned to fire can communicate with it."

Arabelle jotted some numbers in her sketchbook and pretended to study them, but her mind was turning. Communicate with one of the Great Dragons? She had been

at the Battle of the Tower and seen the massive storm dragon
—the White Dragon of England. Deborah Shaw had even
spoken with it. Goose bumps prickled up Arabelle's arms as
she recalled the sheer majesty of the Great Dragon.

"Isn't there a gentleman attuned to fire?" she finally
asked. "Someone more appropriate for such an adventure?"

"None who could make the journey," Phoebe said. "The
roads in Wales are difficult. And you'll find that Lord
Blackerby is blind to social conventions when it comes to
recruiting for his missions."

Arabelle frowned and took a few more measurements.
Lord Blackerby was just another man interested in her for her
dragon—though it was a different sort of interest, at least.
And to speak to a Great Dragon?

She looked up at Eliza. "Why does he need to speak to the
Welsh Dragon? Is it in some danger from Napoleon?"

Eliza and Phoebe shared a glance.

"This is not widely known," Phoebe said slowly, "and you
should keep it to yourself, whatever you decide. But it may
actually be us who are in danger."

"Why?"

"There have been earthquakes in Wales in recent months,"
Eliza said. "The Welsh Dragon appears restless. The Great
Dragons have some awareness of events, even in their deep
sleep. The Red Dragon may be angry because of the attack on
the White Dragon, which is said to be her mate, or because of
the actions of the Luddites or Napoleon. Blackerby wants
to…reassure it."

"There is some risk in approaching the dragon," Phoebe
said. "But you would not go alone, and it is vitally important
to Britain's safety that we try to appease the Red Dragon."

Arabelle looked down at her sketchbook, full of

measurements for Eliza's new dress—measurements she understood, that made up her world. With a focused touch, her magic could reduce the paper to ash.

"It is a wondrous experience to speak to a Great Dragon and hear its voice in your mind," Eliza said, awe tinting her words.

Arabelle closed her sketchbook and looked up at the two women, who watched her expectantly. She now saw concern in their eyes—concern for Arabelle and for themselves and for Britain. But she was not the right person to speak to a Great Dragon—she who scarcely used her magic and did not belong with the dragon-linked of Society. It would be an amazing thing to experience someday, but for now, if the danger was real, then so was the need to find someone already competent.

She hugged the sketchbook to her chest. "You may tell Lord Blackerby I will speak to him."

She would convince him to find someone else to save Britain.

Chapter Five

ARABELLE LOCKED up the shop behind the ladies and paced, walking between lengths of delicate muslin on display and bonnets in need of new ribbons. *That* gown had to be finished in three days, and *that* puce silk was specifically for a countess who was very particular about the hue she wore. Her clients depended on Arabelle.

Except…

Arabelle was very good at helping ladies look their finest, and she loved creating beautiful things with clever designs and careful stitches. *Ackermann's* had been so close to featuring her work, cementing her success. Until that incident with the mob and her fire magic. Her magic—her useless magic and her ineptitude at harnessing it—had almost cost her everything.

Because there were many other dressmakers in London. The truth stuck in her gullet: She needed her clients at least as much as they needed her. Fire magic was powerful, but she couldn't eat it, and it would not keep the rain off her head. She could only be independent of Society by being dependent on Society. She was fortunate Blackerby had chosen to send Phoebe and Eliza to speak to her instead of exerting pressure on her shop—with a few words to the right people, he could probably ruin her livelihood. Maybe he still would.

She wished she could throw a fireball at him if he wanted her magic so much.

A light tap on her door drew her ire. It was clear the shop was closed, especially since it had become so dark outside...

Oh, it was Lord Blackerby.

She steeled herself and opened the door for him and Mr. Farris. And another person: Lord Blackerby's wife, once Lady Amelia and now Lady Blackerby.

"I'm so glad you've condescended to join our little expedition," Lord Blackerby purred.

He walked past Arabelle to make himself comfortable at the table where she consulted with clients. Farris and Amelia both stood to the side, uncomfortable observers.

Blackerby's shadows rolled around him, and Arabelle restrained herself from shooing them away from her fabrics. They were shadows, not smoke; they would not actually harm anything.

She refused to be cowed by the earl. She sat across from him in her usual seat. "I hope to convince you to find someone better suited to this task."

"Which is why we are here," Lord Blackerby said, "to assure you that you are the right person."

"I cannot possibly be the only person attuned to fire in all of Britain."

"You are correct," Lord Blackerby said. "There are three

other dragon-linked persons with fire magic in the country. One is a man so elderly he cannot rise from his bed without assistance. I suppose Farris could carry him up the mountain on his back. The next is a young lady who is on the verge of, uh, taking to bed for a happy occasion. I'm not sure a squalling infant would help our case. And the final is a lad of about ten. He has not yet learned to control his abilities and has a tendency to accidentally set things alight, so he is living at a secluded estate for the time being. Which would you like us to recruit in your place? I own traveling with the incendiary lad would be entertaining."

Arabelle gritted her teeth. "I see the difficulty."

"Come." Lord Blackerby leaned forward and steepled his fingers. "What concerns you? It won't be comfortable, but we'll stay at the most accommodating lodgings possible, and we'll provide a lady's maid for you and the other women—I don't ask you to go unchaperoned."

A lady's maid? A chaperone? What a reminder that Arabelle lived a different life from the rest of them! She contented herself with a cook, a scullery maid, and a girl who served as lady's maid and chambermaid both. Clearly, Lord Blackerby did not understand her situation.

"This is not a good time for me to travel," Arabelle said. "The Season is well underway, and I have many clients to attend to."

Lord Blackerby blinked several times. "The Season? You are worried about your business?"

"Yes!" Now he would understand and leave Arabelle in peace. "It *would* be interesting to speak to a Great Dragon someday—"

"Someday!" Shadows swirled around Lord Blackerby.

"Since Napoleon's escape, there have been disturbances around the world. Storms and earthquakes—we believe fueled by uneasy dragons. The worst triggered a volcano in the Pacific. It filled the sky with ash and wiped out many villages. Our dragon-linked who are attuned to storms say it will disrupt the weather for at least the next year."

"Oh," Arabelle said quietly.

Lord Blackerby went on. "The Red Dragon—a fire dragon —sleeps beneath Dinas Emrys, in Snowdonia, which was formed by ancient volcanos."

A chill raced over Arabelle's skin. "You think our dragon may trigger a volcano? In Britain?"

She could not imagine the destruction. She didn't want to.

Lord Blackerby's posture relaxed. "We hope not. But we must be sure. Not someday. Within the month."

She rubbed her temples. Lord Blackerby was calling her away from everything she built, a house of cards ready to collapse. All so she could do something that sounded impossible. Speak to a Great Dragon. Convince it not to release its wrath on Britain. This was work for some experienced ambassador, not a dressmaker. It was *not* something that she could do best. If she failed…

If she failed, her shop would be the last of her concerns.

"I'm not a…a diplomat," Arabelle said. "I…I have no idea what to wear to meet a Great Dragon!"

Lord Blackerby looked nonplussed by that, and Arabelle felt a moment of satisfaction at throwing him off guard for a change.

Mr. Farris likewise looked perplexed, but Amelia put a hand on her husband's shoulder. She was a quiet lady, and perhaps a little odd—one would have to be to marry Lord

Blackerby—but there was a non-nonsense air about her that Arabelle found comforting.

Amelia smiled softly. "From our limited understanding, it seems the Great Dragons care less about rules of human diplomacy than about the connection that their element gives them to a person. Since you are attuned to fire, this dragon will feel a kinship with you."

Arabelle stared at her, trying to take in the idea of having a kinship with a dragon. She liked Ruby, but her dragon was something of a mystery to her at times.

"I don't think they concern themselves much with human fashion," Amelia went on. "But they seem to enjoy items that might relate to their element. What does your dragon hoard?"

Arabelle glanced at the hearth where Ruby kept his small store of treasures. Lord Blackerby's dark gray dragon was nosing around in the bright objects.

"What is he about?" Arabelle sprang to her feet.

She had never seen one dragon rob another. Yet Lord Blackerby's dragon fetched something from Ruby's hoard and trotted over to the earl with the object in its mouth. Ruby made an annoyed clicking noise and followed.

"Shade only brings me things that harbor secrets." Blackerby smirked at Arabelle and held out his hand for the item.

Yellow flashed in the lamplight, and Arabelle's throat tightened. Why did the blasted dragon have to dig that worthless thing up?

"Citrine," Blackerby said, holding the gem to the light.

Arabelle reached across the table and snatched the gem from Blackerby. "It's amethyst, in fact. But the color was ruined by too much heat."

"Ruined?" Farris blurted out. "It's very interesting."

Arabelle had thought so as well when, as a child, she had first changed the gem's color with her fire magic. Unfortunately, her father, and especially her older brother Tristan—some of London's finest jewelers—had been very clear that it was not *interesting* or *pretty* to waste a purple gem by turning it yellow. No, Tristan hadn't even wanted the worthless stone back. From that day, she had traded the jeweler's shop—and her magical experiments—for her needle. There, her skill left nothing to be ashamed of. It was what she did best, so it was the only thing worth doing.

She returned the stone to Ruby, who scurried over to drop it back in his hoard. He settled on his treasures and huffed at Shade.

"So," Amelia said quickly. "Fire dragons like shiny gems. Perhaps you have a brooch with a fire opal?"

Arabelle considered the jewelry she had—she did like the shimmer of fire opals and owned a few—and as she thought of them, she realized how Amelia had calmed her.

Lord Blackerby grinned at his wife. "Excellent suggestion."

Arabelle sighed. "I still believe I'm more likely to cause problems than solve anything for you. Look at the mess I caused when the Luddites attacked my shop."

"A justified defense of yourself," Lord Blackerby said.

"The fashion magazines didn't think so, and neither did most of London. Also, I was useless when Westminster burned."

"Not at all," Mr. Farris said. "I saw you extinguishing sparks that drifted to other buildings."

Arabelle's eyes widened. He had noticed that? It had been such a small contribution. "But the Parliament building was destroyed! And I almost gave the chaos dragon fire magic at the Battle of the Tower."

"Yet you were able to stop yourself," Lord Blackerby said. "I think you have more control of your magic than you credit yourself with. And besides that, you are the only practical choice."

She shot him a scathing look, but she found the threads of her argument fraying.

"We should be prepared for all types of weather in Wales, especially in spring," Amelia put in.

Her tone was as bland as one might expect when discussing the weather, but she had a keen expression as she steered the conversation onto safer ground.

Arabelle drew a long breath. What did her arguments matter? They would bring every pressure to bear, she would capitulate, and then she would disappoint them. Like her brother, once they saw her fail, they would send her away and leave her alone forever. "Yes, I suppose we will need to pack quite a wardrobe, even if the dragon is not interested in clothing."

"Perhaps I can help you select what to bring," Amelia said, shooting her husband a speaking look.

Arabella wasn't certain what Amelia had in mind, but she would rather deal with the lady than the two men.

"Yes, my dear," Lord Blackerby said with mock humility, though there was real affection in his gaze. "Farris, let us be off. My love, take a carriage home, please."

Amelia smirked at him. "You know I don't fear the dark."

Lord Blackerby tipped his hat to his wife and escorted Farris from the shop.

Arabelle watched them with interest. Who would have

thought Lord Blackerby would find someone who suited him so well?

"Now," Amelia said to Arabelle. "I know my husband can be awkward to work with, but he will keep you safe—all of us safe."

She was so matter-of-fact, it didn't sound like admiration of her husband, but only a statement of truth. Like she was speaking to a friend. But Arabelle had chosen not to be part of the same world as Lady Blackerby.

"Thank you," Arabelle said. "I only hope you will not regret all this trouble."

"I think we will not." Amelia met her eyes. "And the most important thing—you are the only one who can talk to the fire dragon."

"Mrs. Reynolds?" Maria asked, returning from her workspace in the back of the shop. "Was that another client? The sewing girls finished their work and are ready to go home. Oh! I didn't know someone was still here."

"It's fine." Arabelle squished a desire to make certain each stitch was perfect. Apparently, she did not have the time, and Maria *was* competent. Even without Arabelle, she would make her way in the world. The sewing girls, though... Arabelle remembered what it was like to work long into the night as a child, a lamp kept lit by her dragon saving her tired eyes from strain as she sewed. She was careful not to overwork her own young employees. Other dressmakers might not be so generous if Arabelle's shop closed and they had to work elsewhere.

"Yes, the girls may leave for the night. Also..." Arabelle's mouth went dry. She had to force the words out, hardly believing them as she spoke. "I may be going away for a week or so. I will, of course, leave you to oversee everything."

Maria's face lit with excitement, but then her expression fell. "Oh, no. Has someone died?"

Arabelle smiled in spite of herself. "Nothing so drastic. Only…" She glanced at Amelia. "A…friend needs my help."

"Yes, mistress! I won't fail you." Maria bobbed a curtsey and hurried back to relieve the sewing girls from their duties.

"Now," Amelia said. "Let us pack your trunk."

Chapter Six

ARABELLE COULD NEVER HAVE PACKED SUFFICIENTLY for the rain in Wales. The roads seemed little more than rivers of mud, and her poor dragon was miserable with the cold, huddled under her cloak with her in the carriage. Phoebe, sitting across the carriage, looked almost as uncomfortable as Arabelle. She held her dragon in her lap and stroked its back. Eliza sometimes mumbled orders at the rain, and it would let up for a short time only to return later with increased vengeance. The men, riding alongside the carriage, eventually begged her to stop interfering. Only Amelia appeared perfectly content with the slogging pace of the carriage and the weather.

Outside the carriage, Captain Parry was as stoic as one might expect of a sailor, and Lord Westing with his ice magic didn't seem to mind the cold, but Arabelle took a perverse pleasure in noting that Lord Blackerby glowered, his shadows drawn close around him as though darkness could ward off the rain. It wasn't truly his fault that she was on this adventure—assuming that she truly was the only person available attuned to fire who could travel—but she still blamed him.

Farris caught her watching out the window and moved his horse closer. As a Scot, he knew how to dress for wet weather in an oiled coat and wide hat. Arabelle half expected to be scolded for her wicked glee at Blackerby's discomfort, but Farris looked on her with sympathy.

"The weather in Wales takes some getting used to," he said.

"Yes, and I've hardly ever left London." Her shop always needed her, so she'd put off traveling until she felt more confident in its enduring success. "I don't think I've ever seen rain like this."

He nodded. "Take heart. We're nearly to Bodysgallen Hall."

"To where?" Arabelle squinted, trying to see anything through the rain and the green of the trees.

"Bodysgallen Hall, overlooking Conwy," Amelia broke in. "Sir Thomas Mostyn has kindly allowed us the use of his estate."

"He has several," Lord Blackerby grumbled loud enough to be heard in the carriage. "And it will give us a rest from these infernal Welsh roads. Mail toll roads or otherwise, I will inform Prinny we cannot work fast enough to complete improvement projects in Wales. And from Conwy, we still have to ride on to Bangor."

The entire party withered at his comment. Even Farris looked defeated.

Lord Blackerby wagged his finger at them. "I'll hear no complaints. Everyone tells me spring is the most pleasant time in Wales."

Arabelle suspected the earl's sources had failed him in this piece of intelligence. It was hard to imagine a fire dragon living in this climate. Maybe the dragon was attuned to ice or water, and Arabelle was along for nothing. She sighed and leaned back against the seat of the carriage. At least they were nearly to a stopping point where they could get warm and dry.

The carriage wound through green pastures dotted with sheep—a strange sight to Arabelle, who had rarely seen wool in any condition except woven and dyed to bright colors suitable for a warm cloak or pelisse. The hills rolled around them like monstrous waves on the sea and made her feel a little seasick.

If the green hills were the waves of the sea, then Bodysgallen Hall was the lighthouse guiding them. Farris pointed it out to her, but she could not have missed it. The stone walls stood above an ancient forest. Lights burned in the windows, giving Arabelle a sense of borrowed warmth. The house had been built around a central square tower that would offer a commanding view of the bay below, as well as the town and castle ruins at the mouth of the wide river rolling into the bay.

They wound their way up to the front of the house where footmen waited to escort them into their shelter. Arabelle wondered if the servants would flinch from Blackerby's shadows and the other trappings of dragon magic, as she'd heard many in the English countryside did. But the Welsh had always been more pragmatic about their dragons, and the well-schooled footmen did not so much as bat an eye at the crowd of dragons accompanying the guests. Much to Arabelle's relief, the footmen also spoke in English. She had found the Welsh spoken in the roadside inns fascinating but incomprehensible. Blackerby understood it, of course, but the rest of them were left baffled.

They passed through the narrow stone entryway to a cozy hall. Arabelle was surprised on entering the house to find Farris by her side, quick to help her with her traveling cloak.

"The footmen will bring your trunks up to your room," he said. "But perhaps I can show you where you'll be staying?"

"Oh, you've been here before?" she asked.

"Of course. Lord Blackerby sent me to arrange everything."

Arabelle smiled. "I have a sense he'd be lost without you."

A hint of red tinged Farris's ears. "I'm certain he'd muddle on just fine. This is a lovely old house, though. And it has excellent gardens. You might like to see them when the weather clears?"

He sounded almost hopeful. Arabelle had spent little time in gardens, but she did like lovely things. "I would be happy to see them, but I don't know much about gardens, I'm afraid."

"You don't have to know about them to enjoy them. You can see them from your chambers as well. Come, let me show you the way."

Arabelle allowed herself to be led, a little confused by Farris's almost boyish enthusiasm. He must have been very pleased with the arrangements he made for Lord Blackerby. He should not hope to find Arabelle at home in the country, though.

They made their way up the turns of the square staircase past the drawing-room. Arabelle rested her hand on the oak banisters worn smooth by many generations of hands trailing over them. Finally, Farris stopped before a door.

"This one is yours," he announced.

"Thank you."

She swung the door open and paused, taking in the grandeur of the room. She had enjoyed London's finer things during her disastrous Season, yet all but the grandest houses in London were compact. Here, in the country, there was room to stretch out. The room certainly did. The cushioned chairs and large bed draped with heavy curtains to keep the chill away invited her to slow down and relax. A fire crackled merrily in the fireplace, and Arabelle had hopes of being warm and dry once again.

Out the window, she caught a view of the rolling woodlands. The tree's dreary trunks huddled together, closing her out of whatever secrets they hid beneath dripping branches. Her dragon scurried forward, and she followed, drawn to the vista of the distant bay—not like anything she would see in London. Below her, the sunken gardens formed a neat, geometric pattern. It was like the most perfect embroidery but created with living things.

"Oh!" she exclaimed, leaning out to see better. "Like a tapestry. This *is* lovely!"

Perhaps the country was not all bad. She turned back to thank Farris, but he had already vanished.

Arabelle frowned, feeling vaguely disappointed, though she couldn't pin down why. Ruby hopped over and nudged her. She smiled at the little dragon.

"You're ready to make yourself comfortable?"

Arabelle knelt by the hearth and opened the large pouch that held Ruby's hoard. The yellow amethyst twinkled at her in the firelight. She grunted. Why did Ruby have to treasure that reminder of Arabelle's failures? She sighed and turned back to the window.

She would take Farris up on his offer to tour the gardens.

That would show her gratitude for his kindness in trying to help her feel comfortable so far from home. She smiled as she began unpacking her trunks. Warmth spread through her. Well, there was a fire, wasn't there? That would explain the glow deep in her chest.

Chapter Seven

FARRIS HURRIED DOWN THE STAIRS. Blackerby would be quick to help Lady Amelia settle in, and then he would want Farris. Their work here was just beginning, and Farris didn't have time for pleasure. No, the little gasp of happiness from Mrs. Reynolds on seeing the view from her window would have to be enough for him. She clearly disliked being away from the comforts of home, but he hoped she would not be too miserable.

The shadows in the drawing-room were thick. Farris braced himself and stepped inside.

"Fine gardens?" Blackerby drawled from the dimness. "And I thought we chose this place because the tower offers such an opportunity to watch the countryside."

"A lady traveling alone is likely to feel homesick and appreciate the gardens," Farris said, keeping his face and his tone neutral.

"Hmm." Blackerby watched him with a quirk of his lips.

Then, he smiled and stretched out his long frame. "Very well. Let us go to work before you find yourself distracted."

Farris occasionally wished he had time to be distracted— or that anything would distract Blackerby. But that was why Blackerby was so good at what he did. Why England was still safe from enemies at home and abroad.

He followed Blackerby's long strides up the stairs. Past Arabelle Reynolds chambers. Then through a little door that led them to a set of stairs that twisted up and up like the great Tower of Babel the Bible said tried to reach heaven until God confounded men's languages so they could not cooperate for prideful purposes. Farris grunted as the stairs continued upward. Maybe this was that tower, and that was why the Welsh tongue was so confounded confusing, even to a fellow Celtic language speaker.

When they reached the top floor of the tower and threw open the windows, the clouds seemed so close Farris might reach out and brush his fingers through them. The vista below was clear, however. Farris stood, enjoying the views of the distant water. But the shadows around Blackerby were agitated, darting about the tower.

"I don't like it," Blackerby said.

Farris didn't respond. Blackerby enjoyed an audience—he would explain soon enough. Sometimes, Farris wondered if that was the main reason Blackerby kept him around. He would have thought Lady Blackerby would fill that role now, but she didn't take Blackerby overly seriously. That was good for Blackerby—to have someone to keep him grounded when his moods turned too high or low. And it meant Farris still had a role as a listening ear.

"Still no sign of our man Croft," Blackerby said. "And he

was tracking rumors of a threat to the Red Dragon. But the Welsh don't hate dragons. The Luddites have almost no foothold here. Who would have detained Croft?"

"Could some of the Welsh be upset because England is not more friendly to dragons?" Farris asked.

The Scots were a practical people and cared little about dragons unless the creatures impacted them directly. But the Welsh had long been host to the Red Dragon and several other known Great Dragons, and they were proud of their legacy.

Blackerby stared thoughtfully toward the bay. "Certainly, they must understand that we don't welcome the Luddites."

"News travels a long, muddy road to reach these corners of Wales. It might be distorted by the time it arrives."

"Hmm. Perhaps we need a campaign of public relations, then. I had considered keeping our visit to the Red Dragon quiet, but if we presented the journey as a diplomatic mission, it could reassure the Welsh that we respect them and their dragon."

Farris nodded, though diplomacy was not his strong suit. His skills lay more in paying attention and dogged determination.

Blackerby frowned at the harbor below. "Ravens are said to bring news to our White Dragon in London," he mused, almost to himself. "And to the Red Dragon as well. I wonder if she's disturbed by the rumors they whisper into her dreams?"

"That's what we're here to discover, isn't it?" Farris asked.

"Indeed, it is." A wicked grin stole over Blackerby's face. "I hope you weren't planning to sleep tonight. I believe we'll be venturing down to Conwy to befriend some of the locals."

Farris groaned inwardly. He had been looking forward to rest after a long day riding, but there was no arguing with Blackerby. Still, he gave it a half-hearted attempt.

"You're the only one of us who speaks Welsh."

"Nonsense. Firstly, many Welsh in this area speak some English as well. Secondly, everyone speaks more than one language. Parry speaks the language of the sea. Westing and I speak the language of dragons."

"And me?" Farris asked, genuinely curious. This was one of the reasons he liked working for Blackerby—the man always had some insight that surprised him.

"You have something even more important—the ability to watch and listen. I know perfectly well you're capable of reading a man's body language without understanding a word he speaks. It might be the most important skill we've brought with us."

"Thank you, my lord," Farris said, feeling the tips of his ears warm. How rare to receive a sincere word from his master.

Blackerby whirled on him, the mocking humor back in his eyes. "You also have the advantage of being an untitled man who can get his hands dirty. After all, you don't really expect me to walk into a common pub, do you?"

Farris sighed. Blackerby was perfectly willing to walk into a pub if it suited his mood, but the man did dislike getting dirty.

"I assume you mean that literally," Farris said.

Blackerby smiled. "Of course I do. Prepare to try the virtues of common Welsh ale. I understand it's quite palatable. The Welsh need something to help them through this miserable cold."

"Yes, my lord," Farris said, repressing a smirk. If Blackerby thought this was cold, he needed to spend more time in Scotland.

"Have no fear. I'll send Parry with you. He is, after all, more congenial company than Westing."

Farris had no argument there.

Chapter Eight

"If our goal is to be inconspicuous, I'm afraid I'm a hindrance," Captain Parry said as he strolled beside Farris toward the ferry crossing for Conwy.

Farris chuckled. "I'm not exactly unnoticeable myself."

The former captain limped slightly, owing to his false leg, and his eye patch was certainly not inconspicuous. Furthermore, his wife had urged her dragon to accompany them, arguing that the Welsh would take more kindly to them with a dragon along. The creature was perched on Parry's shoulder, knocking his hat askew as its head slithered this way and that to watch the new terrain.

But Farris was used to looming over everyone. Blackerby was almost his height, and he sometimes suspected the earl stretched a bit to avoid feeling like Farris had any advantage over him.

Farris clapped Parry on the back. "You'll still mix in better than Lord Westing."

Parry laughed at that. "True enough. I can't imagine

Blackerby and Westing mingling with the common folk. I suppose their role is to hobnob with the elite of Conwy, leaving us with the riffraff."

"That's the plan," Farris said, trying to imagine icy Lord Westing enjoying a pint with the locals.

"You'll not hear me complain," Parry said. "Our task is more enjoyable."

"That it is!" Farris could deal with the gentry when he had to—his father had been a well-off engineer—but he found Society and all of its ins and outs tiring.

They reached the crossing, and Parry fell into an easy conversation with the—thankfully bilingual—ferryman. Farris let his mind and gaze wander to the prominent nearby hills. The ruins of Deganwy Castle in particular caught his attention. Blackerby had warned that the hill it stood upon was an extinct volcano—one of many in Britain that might be reactivated by an angry fire dragon. But why was the Welsh dragon angry? The ferryman was enchanted with Mrs. Parry's dragon—the rough-looking man cooing at it like a child with a kitten.

The ferry deposited them on the other side, and Farris studied the ruins of Conwy Castle—the English answer to the Welsh stronghold of Deganwy across the estuary. On their other side rose Mynydd y Dref—another ancient volcano towering over the tiny town, ready to crush it if anything ever reawakened its fires.

"What's troubling you?" Parry asked.

Farris shrugged. "Just wondering why people choose to live in such a far-flung place. It's not easy to reach. Imagine the difficulty in bringing food and supplies along those roads. Yet people have been here for centuries—even fighting over it." He gestured to the opposing castles.

Parry gawked at him for a moment, then burst into laughter. "Spoken like a landlubber!"

Now it was Farris's turn to gawk.

Parry grinned. "Look at this port! It's lovely. A quick sail to Ireland or England. Oh, I grant you, the waters here can be rough, but if you stop thinking like you're tied to roads and horses, it isn't so isolated at all. Buy yourself some land in that little village on the shore down there—I'd wager the place is going to grow, especially with the improved roads Blackerby is going on about." His smile faded. "As long as the dragon doesn't destroy it, I suppose. But that's why we're here, right?"

Farris nodded and led the way up Conwy's wide, packed-dirt High Street. Ahead, the Dutch-style stepped façade of the ancient Plas Mawr looked down on its neighbors. Several public houses and inns greeted them with oil lights, scents of cooking mutton and cheese, the sounds of laughter, and… was that a harp?

Farris grinned and pointed to a swinging sign advertising The Harp Inn. "That's our spot—a posting inn. It looks popular with the folks traveling the road and the locals. Flowing with ale and gossip. And the Welsh are famous for their harp music, aren't they?"

Mrs. Parry's dragon flapped its wings and nuzzled his ear as if in agreement.

"Can't argue with that," Parry said.

The Harp Inn wasn't much different from an English posting inn—the scent of food mingling with the dust and sweat of the male bodies crowded inside while a fire crackled in the hearth. The centerpiece, however, was the man playing the harp. Farris was more used to seeing ladies playing tall, dainty harps, but this harp was squatter and more curved, and the man playing it clearly did not think it a feminine pursuit. The music, too, was different, a tune that pulled at Farris's Scottish heart. The Welsh and Scots were ancient neighbors, after all. He wondered what these folks would think of a set of pipes playing a reel.

Parry left Farris's side and quickly fell in with a group of seafaring men. Farris ordered a drink and a dish with an unpronounceable name—which turned out to be a soup with leeks and cheese that was warming and delicious.

Farris nursed his ale, wanting to keep his mind clear. Parry gestured with his drink while he exchanged stories with his new sailor friends, but Farris noted he never drank from it. Good man, keeping his head about him. While Parry provided entertainment and distraction with his tall tales of the sea, Farris withdrew into the shadows—a trick he could manage despite his size, though never as well as Lord Blackerby might—and watched the crowd. Some of the men were there on business—a necessary stop between England and the western Welsh coast and on to Ireland. They ate and drank methodically and made their way upstairs to their rooms for sleep. Others were clearly local—English heavily accented if they spoke it at all, and with time to pass in the public house.

But there was another class of men present that Farris couldn't pin down. Like him, they clung to the shadows, and they watched Parry—or at least the dragon he fed from his plate of mutton—with keen interest disguised as fleeting glances. Not everyone in Wales was a friend of dragons, then.

Farris stood, pretending to stagger a little as he made his way toward the barkeep. He bumped into one of the reclusive men.

"Oh, sorry friend!" Farris said, tipping his hat drunkenly.

The man only grunted and scooted farther from Farris.

Hmm. Interesting. Farris couldn't learn if the man was English or Welsh if he wouldn't speak.

"Oh, did I spill on your coat? Many apologies!" Farris sloshed his drink for good effect.

The man snarled and stood to stomp away.

Was the man deliberately hiding his voice? That worried Farris even more.

He finished his errand, replacing his spilled drink with a fresh one. He kept all his senses trained on the lurking strangers, but the rest of them left soon after the man he had bumped into. Had he given too much away? Confound it all. Maybe they had moved to another public house—one of the quieter ones out of the way.

Parry must have noted Farris's unease because he finished his story with a flourish and stood to say goodbye to his new friends.

Farris followed him out into the street.

"You found something," Parry whispered.

"Only something we need to investigate further."

Parry grunted and stumbled. Farris thought for a moment the captain had tripped on the uneven road. Then, a blade flashed on the edge of his vision.

Farris stepped aside and leveled a blow with his elbow at the masked man who had crept up behind him.

"Brigands!" Farris yelled.

Parry's attacker swung a punch at Parry that dropped him to the ground, then rushed forward to help his fellow against Farris.

"Thieves!" Farris shouted, trying to be heard over the harp and chatter from the inn. "Attackers!"

The two men circled him. As he suspected, they were two

of the men from the pub. Where were the others? He tried to move to keep them both in sight, but they were quick and coordinated. He took a glancing blow to the side of his head and staggered back.

Something rushed past him, and he thought the man had swung a sword. But it was Mrs. Parry's dragon. The water dragon shrieked and spewed boiling water on the assailants.

The men howled in agony and tore away shirts now drenched in steaming hot water. This commotion was finally enough to draw attention, and men rushed from the inn to see what the fuss was about.

The onlookers were rewarded with the sight of two half-dressed villains rushing off into the darkness, Farris panting and holding his hands up to defend himself, and the dragon whooshing about the street. Parry raised himself to a sitting a position and checked on his false leg.

There was a great deal of hubbub in Welsh, which Farris recognized as general calls of alarm and a rush to find the magistrate and pursue the escaping villains. Blackerby was right: some things did not need translation.

Someone asked him something, garbled either because of the pulse still hammering in his ears or the different language, and he could only manage. "No."

No, he didn't know who attacked him. No, he wasn't seriously hurt. No, he didn't understand.

That seemed good enough for the crowd, who dispersed in the excitement of the manhunt. Farris wanted to ask if anyone knew who the men had been, but that would have to wait.

He turned instead to offer a hand up to Captain Parry.

The captain rose shakily, adjusting his balance on his false leg. "At least they didn't damage it this time. You can't imagine how difficult it is to find a comfortable leg."

The dragon circled Parry, screeched again, and flew off to the east, toward Bodysgallen.

"Oh, that's not good," Parry said.

"Why?" Farris asked. "What's wrong?"

"That treacherous creature has no doubt gone back to tell my wife that I have been stabbed."

"Stabbed!"

Farris checked, and indeed, blood oozed down Parry's back.

"We need to find a physician!"

Parry laughed a little unevenly. "Physician. That's difficult to say even in English. Do you know the Welsh word for it?"

"I think this is one of Blackerby's universal languages."

"Well, you'd best have the physician meet us as Bodysgallen, because I'm more afraid of my wife in a rage than any amount of blood loss."

Farris hesitated.

Parry gripped his arm. "Come. The wound isn't a fatal one, and we have information to convey."

The ground rumbled, rattling the window panes of the buildings around them. Another earthquake.

Farris's chest tightened, and he looked up to the ancient volcano looming over the city. It had slept since mankind had settled on these shores. But the dragon had slept many centuries as well.

What was happening in Wales?

Chapter Nine

A SLAMMING door jolted Arabelle from sleep. Silence followed, eerie for its lack of carriages rattling over streets or watchmen calling the hour. How anyone managed to rest in the deathly stillness of the country, she would never know. Footsteps sounded in the corridor, and a raised female voice, muffled by the thick door, called something. She swung her bed curtains aside, but it was still the thick darkness of deep night. The damp cold rushed in around her, chilling her face, and she was tempted to crawl under her covers and ignore whatever commotion was taking place down the corridor. It was unlikely to concern her.

But Ruby hopped up from his place by the hearth with a worried twittering and paced to the door.

That banished her last hopes for a peaceful night. Ruby wouldn't have stirred for something simple like a call for more warming pans or a domestic disagreement. She threw on her dressing gown and hurried out, her dragon prancing along beside her.

In the drawing-room, she found the lamps lit and the ladies gathered in the quavering yellow light. The other women hardly noted Arabelle's presence. Eliza Parry paced, one hand held protectively on her rounded belly, and her dragon scurrying along the floor to keep up with her. Phoebe stood wringing her fingers, little flickers of light twitching above her head. Only Amelia looked calm as she watched out the window.

"I'm certain we will know soon enough what has happened," Amelia said.

"My dragon would not have returned except to alert me to danger," Eliza said. "And look! There is blood on her talons!"

Arabelle saw the dark stains and shivered. When the mob had attacked her shop, Ruby had spit fire at them, but she'd never seen a dragon physically attack someone.

"Do we go looking for the men, then?" Phoebe asked. "That seems more likely to cause confusion."

"No need," Amelia said. "A carriage approaches. Well, a wagon, at best, I believe."

Eliza raced down the stairs to the front landing and pulled the door open. The other ladies followed, though Arabelle hung back, feeling like an intruder. In the light spilling from the door, Arabelle could just make out Farris's red hair. He hopped down from the wagon and helped someone out. Captain Parry, leaning heavily on him. He did have that false leg. But no, his legs both seemed intact—he was too unsteady to walk.

"What happened!" Eliza demanded, rushing forward.

"Just a little cut, my love," Captain Parry said slowly, stumbling over the words. "Farris here told the ferryman to send a surgeon to Bodysgallen. Confound it, there's nothing to be so concerned about. Though, it's so blasted cold..."

"He's losing blood," Farris said. "I poured some strong whiskey over the cut to draw out any infection, and I staunched it with a handkerchief, but we have to stop the bleeding."

They stood in silence for a moment. None of them were surgeons, and it would take some time for anyone to come from the town.

"Mrs. Reynolds is an expert with a needle," Amelia said.

Arabelle's breath caught, and she held her hands up to ward off the idea. "I can stitch fabric. I've never stitched up a person before."

The thought made her queasy. Blood and skin and muscles, and she couldn't unpick the stitches and reset her work as if a person were a sleeve.

Farris stepped nearer. "Pretend it's just a tear in a gown. Work quickly and neatly, and Captain Parry will thank you later."

Farris looked at her with such faith that it softened the hard lump of dread in her chest. But he was not the one who would have to do the stitching.

Arabelle glanced at the others. Tears welled in Eliza's eyes as she clasped her husband's hand. He did look very pale.

Ruby bumped her leg. Arabelle scooped him up, and the dragon nestled into her arms, nudging her chin with his head. Farris squeezed her arm gently, and the warmth of his confidence rushed through her. It was only sewing, after all. She could sew in her sleep.

"Very well. I will do it."

Eliza shot her a look of gratitude, and Farris nodded.

Parry groaned. "I'm going to need more of that whiskey. Or opium if any's to be found."

"What can I do?" Eliza asked.

"Just stay with him, if you don't mind the blood," Farris said.

She straightened her shoulders. "Of course I don't!"

Farris gestured to Phoebe. "Bring him a strong drink and something to bite down on. Some vinegar as well. Mrs. Reynolds, your needles?"

She nodded and rushed to grab them from her room. She chose her sharpest one, feeling a great deal of pity for Captain Parry.

They had moved him to one of the bedchambers, and he lay prone on the mattress with his upper clothes removed. Phoebe looked extremely embarrassed, glancing everywhere but at Captain Parry. Arabelle was unphased. She had seen enough ladies in states of undress that a man's back was hardly shocking to her.

Farris held a cloth against the wound in Parry's lower back. Red bloomed through the white fabric.

"You're fortunate," Farris said to Parry, whose eyes were glazed with the numbing effects of whiskey or opium. "It missed the kidney and the intestines."

At that image, a wave of dizziness hit Arabelle, and she almost fled the room. But Farris locked eyes with her and beckoned her over, his gaze keeping her steady.

"Clean the needle and thread in vinegar," he said matter-of-factly. "It will help the wound heal."

Phoebe held out the vinegar for Arabelle, who took a deep breath and dipped her instruments in the sharp-scented liquid. It was only sewing. She did it every day. She was *good* at it.

She tried not to watch as Farris wiped the wound clean and then held it closed. He motioned with his head for Arabelle to join him. She shuffled over to stand beside Farris, comforted by the sturdiness of his presence and his faith in her. As if she could lean on him when she felt dizzy and he would catch her. She lifted her needle, her hands trembling slightly. No. That would not do. She was only stitching a torn bodice—no skin, no muscle, no blood.

She took a deep breath and went to work. Neat little stitches to repair the *bodice* so no one would ever know it had torn.

Having to pause to wipe the blood off her needle did not help the illusion.

Thankfully, while Captain Parry groaned and clamped his jaw on the stick, he did not writhe or cry out. She could not have born that.

She finished the last stitch, cut the thread, and stepped back, taking in the line of stitches now closing Captain Parry's back. Her knees went wobbly, and this time, Farris did catch her. His arm wrapped around her waist, and she leaned her head against his chest as he helped her to a chair.

"You did excellent!" he said, beaming at her.

She managed a shaky smile in return. "I...I'm glad I could help."

Eliza had barely begun fussing over her husband when the sound of horses' hooves sounded from the drive.

A few moments later, Lord Blackerby burst into the room, shadows swarming around him. Lord Westing followed, with presumably the surgeon in tow, given the stains on the man's coat. Arabelle wrinkled her nose at the surgeon's dirty appearance. She would not wish to be attended to by someone still bearing traces of his last encounter.

"What happened?" Lord Westing rushed to Phoebe, who stood to the side, her face pale. "We met the physician coming this way. Did someone attack the house?"

"It happened in Conwy," Farris said. "The captain insisted on returning here."

The surgeon pushed his way forward and stood over Parry.

"Not what I would have advised," he said in heavily accented English. He studied Arabelle's stitches and grunted. "You have done passable work, though I am half tempted to redo the stitches."

Parry groaned.

"You will not!" Eliza said. "He's been through enough."

"I don't think anyone could have done that better than Mrs. Reynolds," Farris said quietly.

Arabelle flushed with pleasure.

The surgeon grunted again and looked to Lord Blackerby. "I still expect to be paid for the trouble of coming all the way out here."

Lord Blackerby sneered and tossed him a coin. "Leave the laudanum. The good captain will need it. If you are wise, you will now remove yourself more quickly than you came."

The surgeon didn't need any further warning. Eliza was happy to take the laudanum from him.

"Now, my dears," Lord Blackerby said. "You had a much more eventful night than Westing and I. Tell me about it."

"Shouldn't Parry rest?" Eliza demanded.

"Yes," Lord Blackerby said. "And the sooner I hear all, the sooner he can."

Farris quickly launched into a description of their evening, including the attack.

Arabelle listened with growing unease. What had seemed

at first a rather far-fetched excursion now loomed as dangerous and *real*. She was facing enemies who were willing to kill. She was not a soldier or a pugilist—only a seamstress. She could lose everything.

The Luddite attack on her shop came fresh again to her mind. She had fended them off with fire—perhaps feeding into their desire to show that the dragon-linked could be dangerous—but she had been so angry. So frightened. That shop was her life. What was she without it?

"A very eventful evening indeed," Lord Blackerby said thoughtfully when Farris finished his account. "They were careful not to speak in front of you, so they knew it would give something away."

"You know..." Parry slurred from the table. "I thought I heard one of them swear in French when the dragon scalded him."

"Do you speak French?" Lord Blackerby asked.

Parry chuckled hoarsely, then winced. "I'm a sailor. I know how to swear in nearly every language. I'd challenge any accomplished young lady or Oxford scholar to rival the breadth of my language training." The words came out in a sleepy murmur.

Eliza smiled and stroked his shoulder gently. "Yes, dear. We're very proud."

"Though not Welsh," he mumbled. "Does Welsh sound like French? I should learn a Welsh word or two while I'm here."

"I think you should sleep," Eliza said.

"No doubt," Lord Blackerby agreed. "Though that's an angle we will have to consider. The French. Hmm."

The shadows swirled around him, revealing a distress that the Home Secretary didn't allow to cross his expression.

Arabelle understood their agitation. This was far outside of her experience. The most she knew of the French was about their fashions and whatever she read in the newspapers. Captain Parry probably knew more of the language than she did.

As they exited Parry's new bedchamber, she noticed Farris dabbing his handkerchief at his head. It came away with spots of blood.

"You're injured, too!" she exclaimed.

Farris gave a guilty start, and Lord Blackerby eyed him.

"Nothing serious!" Farris said. "A glancing blow to the head."

"We ought at least to clean it up." Arabelle thought of him helping others and ignoring his own injury, and her impulse was to fuss over him much as Eliza fussed over her captain.

"Indeed," Lord Blackerby said. "Sir Thomas would be upset if we bloodied any of the furniture. I'm certain Mrs. Reynolds can attend to you as well as she did Captain Parry."

Arabelle warmed with pride. She had done a respectable job. Who would have guessed it?

"I don't think my head needs to be stitched," Farris objected weakly.

"But I can look at it, at least," Arabelle said. "It's not as if you can examine your own scalp."

She wasn't certain why Lord Blackerby looked so smug over the arrangement, or why he seemed anxious to usher everyone else away. Maybe Farris's wound was more serious than she thought.

Chapter Ten

ARABELLE SPARED no worry for being alone with Farris. It wouldn't have been proper for a young Society girl, but with Farris and her, it only felt comfortable. She directed him to a chair, and he allowed himself to be led.

"Come, Mr. Farris. Sit down here where there is light."

Even with her limited experience of injuries, though, she could see that the bump and shallow cut were more likely painful than dangerous.

She dabbed it clean, and Farris didn't flinch.

"You'd best use the vinegar if you're going to do it properly, I suppose," Farris said.

"Won't it hurt?"

Farris glanced up at her. "Have no fear of hurting me, Mrs. Reynolds. I'm a stout-hearted Scot"

"I suppose you would have to be to work for Lord Blackerby."

He chuckled. "He's not the easiest to work for."

"But you admire him."

"I do. He's a tricky one, but he has to be for the threats we face. And you'll not find anyone so loyal, despite the front he puts on. Some of that is for dealing with Society."

"They're difficult, are they not?" Arabelle laughed.

"You could have joined them, but you chose not to," Farris said questioningly.

"True. I did not like being valued for my dragon and nothing else."

"Someone would have to be a fool to only value you for your dragon."

Arabelle's face warmed at the words. "That's very kind of you, but I'm afraid it was the way of that world. My dragon or my needle—those were my only options, and you know which I chose. I do occasionally miss the dancing and all the glittering color and even magic of it. But I suppose I would have outgrown that anyway."

"You speak as if you're a gray-haired matron," Farris said. "And even them I have sometimes seen enjoying a lively dance. Many a Scottish matriarch can still dance a reel."

Arabelle laughed, but there was no heart in it. "No doubt true. Maybe someday I will have time again for dancing."

"Why wait?" Farris asked.

Arabelle hesitated over his question. She had enjoyed dancing. She hated to think she had let some shallow-minded men ruin something she liked doing. But it was more than that. If she was dancing or attending parties, she wasn't working in her shop. "It seems a waste of time, I suppose."

"Enjoying yourself is a waste?"

"I enjoy sewing!"

"I know. I've seen you at work. But does that mean you can only enjoy sewing?"

"It's the only thing I'm really skilled at."

"I'll never believe you're a poor dancer," Farris said, a hint of teasing in his voice.

"No, I'm not! But dancing is…not important. Outside of the Season, no one cares if you can dance."

"Why do you care if they care? Why not do something just for yourself?"

Arabelle stared down at the cloth clutched in her hands, but what she saw was her brother's look of disgust when she ruined his amethyst with her fire magic. She recalled eavesdropping and hearing her so-called suitors laughing about her connection to trade. She thought of the writers at *Ackermann's* suddenly unwilling to talk to her after she used her magic to defend her shop. Why bother dancing, or practicing magic, or doing anything else, really, when the only thing that gave her any creditability was her ability as a dressmaker? It was dangerous to step outside her narrow realm, and she was not welcome there. If she could know she was secure in her reputation as a dressmaker—if *Le Belle Assemblée* or some other arbiter of fashion would proclaim her position—maybe then she could relax and think of something else.

She looked away from Farris's expectant gaze and shook her head. "Perhaps someday. When I know my shop is secure. I have to keep clients coming to me for their gowns. After I used magic against the Luddites, some have been hesitant."

"Magic is acceptable, though."

"In ladies and lords. Not in women keeping shops. I'm… an anomaly. It makes people uncomfortable."

"That's ridiculous! You're a fine dressmaker, and they all know it. Your magic shouldn't matter one way or the other."

Arabelle warmed at his earnestness. "I think you must be loyal as well as stout-hearted."

"For the right cause, I would move mountains."

Arabelle finished cleaning the wound, glad to see it was not bleeding seriously anymore. Yet she did not want the conversation with Farris to end.

"Was that why you came to London? Why you work for Lord Blackerby?"

"My father wanted me to be an engineer like him. I did like solving problems, but even working outdoors, I felt restless. Trapped by the narrowness of the problem to be solved. Blackerby took notice of me when I worked on a project for the Prince Regent, and he offered me more interesting problems to solve."

"I would imagine, in engineering, you were less likely to be cudgeled."

"True." He chuckled. "But I also had few opportunities to work with lovely and interesting ladies."

Something tightened around Arabelle's chest, like a corset laced too snug. As charming and handsome as Farris was, she should have guessed he was surrounded by admiring women. "Oh. Does Lord Blackerby have you working with many ladies, then?"

He grinned. "Only you."

Arabelle's heart skipped at his words. He thought her lovely and interesting? How long had it been since anyone had called her lovely? Her designs, yes. But herself, rarely.

Farris's gaze locked with hers, and he stood slowly. He suddenly seemed very close, but Arabelle didn't back away.

"Thank you for your ministrations, Mrs. Reynolds." He cleared his throat. "Perhaps I could do something for you in return?"

She blinked and looked at the window still showing the velvet blackness of night. "Right now?"

"Why put it off? You said you missed dancing, and I'm not such a poor partner."

Arabelle's face heated, and she lowered her eyes so she found herself staring at Farris's broad chest. "I doubt we could find a piper to play us a reel."

"No." There was a smile in his voice. "But I know more than just the reel. Do you hear the clock ticking?"

She paused to listen, found its quiet rhythm, then nodded.

"Do you waltz, Mrs. Reynolds?"

"Oh, I...I learned once, but..." But she wasn't very good. Yet when she met Farris's eyes again, that didn't seem to matter. "I will try."

He smiled, put one hand gently on her waist while taking her hand with his other, and led her into the rhythm of the dance. Arabelle resisted for a few beats, trying to remember the steps on her own, but then she relaxed and let Farris lead. They spun about the room several times, their movements in perfect harmony, though Arabelle no longer knew if they were keeping time with the clock or only with each other.

Farris brought them to a stop, and they stood in the lamplight, staring at each other, the moment shimmering and fragile like the most delicate gauze. Arabelle was afraid even to breathe too deeply in case she rent it to mere threads.

Finally, Farris sighed and lowered his hands.

"I must get back to Lord Blackerby. Thank you for the dance, Mrs. Reynolds."

With a bow, he retreated, leaving a flustered Arabelle to watch him go, wondering if she could pull those threads together again.

Chapter Eleven

FARRIS PRACTICALLY SKIPPED down the stairs, not really seeing his path, his mind full of how pretty Arabelle Reynolds looked when she flushed. And she had flushed for him. Was it possible she shared even a glimmer of the interest in him that he felt for her?

She had a dragon. She could have reached for the highest echelons of Society. Even without a dragon, she would always have been far above Farris. It was like longing for the moon in her progress across the night. Farris was only a Bow Street Runner. The son of an engineer, true, which was respectable enough, but not ever able to ascend so high as Arabelle Reynolds could. Even now, Society would reluctantly embrace her if she chose to leave her shop. Farris would embrace her much more willingly if she thought him worthy. He would find a way to make himself worthy.

"And how fares your head?" Blackerby asked when Farris found him in the drawing-room. Was he smirking a little?

"Fine as a fiddle," Farris responded.

Blackerby was definitely smirking. "Get a few hours rest nonetheless. You're no good to me if your mind is muddled. Then, we must apply ourselves to the problem of French swearing."

"Captain Parry lost a great deal of blood, and he'd taken whiskey."

"But if the French are in Wales…the danger is too great to ignore the possibility."

"The Welsh like dragons," Farris said.

"Yes, but they don't like English. Welsh miners and ironworkers are essential to the war effort, yet they are underpaid and ridiculed by their English counterparts. And Prinny's toll roads are expensive for locals who don't have the money that the post coach or gentleman travelers are willing to pay for better roads. No, the French in Wales would be very dangerous. And if they are tampering in some way with the Red Dragon…"

"I see," Farris said.

And he did, very clearly. No time for thoughts of pretty ladies. He went to his chamber and fell into a heavy sleep, and if he dreamed of dancing in the moonlight with Arabelle Reynolds, he did not let it distract him from his duties when he woke.

In fact, he reached the breakfast table before Blackerby did. The Home Secretary joined him soon, however, looking chipper.

"No need to be smug about beating me here," Blackerby said, helping himself to the sausages. "My wife insisted I take my own advice and rest as well."

"She is a wise woman," Farris said, hiding his smirk behind a cup of tea.

A smile played on Blackerby's lips. "Indeed, she is." His smile faded. "And she's in danger like the rest of us if we don't solve this riddle."

That wiped away Farris's smile as well. If he wanted to be worthy of Arabelle Reynolds, he ought to at least make certain she was not killed. "Yes. my lord. Where do we start?"

"The direct approach, this time."

"Ah."

Blackerby's direct approach could be…terrifying—there was really no other term for it. But it was effective.

They took horses to the ferry. The ferryman watched them with curiosity, no doubt realizing that these recent passengers brought interest to Conwy.

"Do you have many French travelers this way?" Blackerby asked, tossing the man a guinea.

The ferryman gawked at the golden coin, then looked at Blackerby, obviously wondering what his lordship wanted to hear.

"The truth, please," Blackerby said smoothly.

The ferryman pocketed the coin. "Occasionally, my lord. It's mostly English and Welsh. Sometimes the Irish."

"Recently, though?" Blackerby pressed.

The ferryman looked thoughtful. "I did think I heard some French talk the other day. Mind you, I don't speak that heretic language, but it sounded like French to me. They paid in good English money, though."

Blackerby nodded, his expression grim. "Thank you."

Once they reached Conwy, they stabled their horses at The Harp Inn, and Blackerby strode into the establishment, shadows swirling about him, and his dragon perched on his shoulder. The creature spread its wings, giving Blackerby the silhouette of some dark angel.

The inn was mostly empty at that time of day—just a few men probably waiting for the post coach. All eyes went to Blackerby, just as the earl intended. The innkeeper rushed forward, bowing low in deference to Blackerby's obvious status and wealth.

"My lord! A room for the night?"

"No." Blackerby took out a guinea and rolled it over his knuckles. "I'm here to find out more about your French customers."

The innkeeper glanced between the guinea and the shadows creeping out across the floor of his establishment. The other guests quickly looked to their cold ham and meat pies and ale, but they watched from the corners of their eyes.

"I... Many customers come through here my lord. I don't always know..."

"Are you saying you've never served any Frenchmen in your inn?" Blackerby pressed.

The innkeeper's Adam's apple bobbed. "I, uh..."

Farris took pity on the man and stepped forward. "It's not illegal to serve Frenchmen, of course. You're just doing your duty as a host. But we have a duty as well. We're tracking certain Frenchmen who may have come through here recently."

The innkeeper relaxed and mopped his brow. "Of course, of course! I'm certain we sometimes have French customers. I'm trying to recall..."

"The men last night were French," came a quiet voice from beside the hearth. The harper sat in the shadows, tuning his instrument. "The ones who started the fight in the street. They were cagey about it, but I heard them."

"Excellent work," Blackerby said.

The harper bowed his head, a glint in his eyes. "To some, I'm only part of the furnishings. It makes it easy to be overlooked—and to overhear things."

"And you overheard things last night?" Blackerby asked. "You understand French?"

"I studied several languages in my training, my lord, French among them. Yes, the men were not speaking very openly, but I caught something about a dragon."

"The Red Dragon?" Blackerby asked, his eyes sharp.

"Uh, no, I think they meant the dragon that sailor fellow had as a companion. They meant to make an example of him."

Farris groaned to himself. The dragon wasn't even Parry's! But it had served to draw out some enemies. As long as Parry's wound did not become infected, he would likely consider it worthwhile.

Blackerby nodded. "Did they capture those men?"

"No, my lord," the innkeeper said quickly. "The night watch searched, but there was no sign of them."

Blackerby swore under his breath. He tossed a guinea to the innkeeper and another to the harper. "Thank you for your time."

Farris followed him into the streets. "Was it just a crime of opportunity, then? They hate magic and wanted to hurt someone they thought had a dragon?"

"What do you think?" Blackerby asked, his expression neutral.

"I doubt it. Why draw attention to themselves in such a way if they didn't have some deeper motives?"

"I agree. We must find these ruffians. To the docks."

"The docks?"

"The easiest way out of the city. Would you recognize the men again if you saw them? Could you describe them to a stranger?"

"Yes, my lord. I might even be able to sketch them— engineer's training."

Blackerby smiled grimly. "Excellent. Do it."

Luckily, they were at a posting inn. Farris went back inside for some discarded paper and sketched the two men he'd seen clearly. Not so good a sketch as a skilled young lady might have produced for her governess, but passable.

Blackerby studied the pictures, then motioned for Farris to follow him to the docks. Blackerby presented the sketch to every person he could find. A few balked at the sight of this London-polished gentleman with his shadows and his dragon ordering them around, but when he repeated his questions in Welsh, they all answered. Some looked thoughtful, others quickly shook their heads no. None had seen the Frenchmen, it seemed.

"My lord!" The ferryman puffed up to Blackerby. "My lord, you were asking after Frenchmen?"

"Yes, have you seen them?"

"I have, my lord. I just gave them a ride across the river."

Blackerby snatched the paper from Farris's hand. "These French men?"

"Yes, my lord. Those two plus one other man."

"And you took them across the river?" Blackerby snarled.

"I didn't know you wanted me to stop them." The ferryman quaked. "They headed that way."

He pointed toward Bodysgallen.

Farris stepped forward. "You told us; that's the important thing. And now we'll need you to take us after them." He looked to Blackerby. "It can't be a coincidence that they headed toward Bodysgallen when we started asking about them."

Blackerby set his lips in a thin line, and shadows darted away from him toward the house where his wife and the other women waited. "Get the horses!"

Chapter Twelve

ARABELLE WAS GRATEFUL FOR EMBROIDERY—OTHERWISE, she wouldn't have known what to do with herself. The other ladies invited her to have tea with them—insisted on it, even. But this was too strange. They were her clients. True, if she had chosen, she could have been part of the *beau monde*, but she had turned her back on it. Yet there she sat, a dressmaker sipping tea with Lady Phoebe Westing, Lady Amelia Blackerby, and the fabulously wealthy Mrs. Eliza Parry as they discussed all the latest novels.

"You have read *Mansfield Park*, of course," Eliza said to Arabelle.

Arabelle's cheeks warmed, and she kept her eye on her needle. "I have heard clients debating its merits, but I have not yet read it."

"Not everyone enjoys reading novels, and that is no defect," Phoebe said quickly. "There are other ways to fill one's mind."

How kind of her to try to cover for what must seem a

shortcoming to them. Arabelle met Phoebe's gaze. "I do like to read, but I find I only have time for fashion magazines. Most of my time is spent in sewing or sketching new designs."

"Naturally!" Phoebe's eyes brightened. "And you are so talented at it."

Arabelle murmured her gratitude, her needle slowing. "I don't recall when I stopped having time for novels."

They had become another thing that she put aside for later. Like dancing. Like magic. Like love. Her shop had to be successful for her to survive, of course, but a worry pricked at her that she was only surviving and not living. But perhaps that was just the influence of taking tea with those above her station—making her think she could afford luxuries that were out of her reach.

"I will loan you my copy of *Mansfield Park*," Eliza said.

"Oh, I would enjoy reading it, but I may not have time—"

"You can return it whenever you find the time." Eliza sipped her tea, ending the debate.

"I did not like Fanny Price nearly as much as Elizabeth Bennet," Phoebe said.

"She is not as strong-willed," Amelia put in quietly, "but she had a different form of strength honed to help her survive a soft, slow kind of unhappiness."

Arabelle knew little of Amelia, but she sensed the lady had experienced her own soft, slow unhappinesses. At least she seemed content with Lord Blackerby.

"Well, whatever the identity of the lady who writes these novels, she knows something of the problems of the West Indies," Eliza said. "I believe she has connections to naval men, perhaps a husband or brother."

Amelia nodded. "When one writes, one is always observing her surroundings for story material."

Arabelle darted a quick, curious glance at Amelia. The lady—now a countess—had never publicly acknowledged her alleged role as the scandalous authoress Miss Charity, and her marriage to Lord Blackerby had both cemented her place in public gossip and raised her above it.

"The lady must have a dragon as well," Phoebe added. "Her descriptions of Edmund's earth magic were excellent."

"I wonder what she might be attuned to," Eliza said, staring thoughtfully at her cucumber sandwich. "Surely, it must influence her writing."

Amelia kept her eyes on the chain of stitches in front of her. Her magic didn't influence her work. How could it help her when it always wanted to escape her control? She wondered if the mysterious authoress felt the same, or if the lady had somehow managed to turn her magic to an atypical pursuit.

The three dragons in the room perked up from their various napping and exploring to stare at the doorway. Amelia's chest tightened at their alertness, but then Lord Westing passed in the corridor, and the dragons relaxed. Lord Westing paused long enough to give his wife a surprisingly warm smile, then continued on his patrol. He probably wanted to be out there with Lord Blackerby and Farris, but Arabelle was grateful he'd been left behind. The house was so large. So isolated.

Phoebe rang for more tea, and the ladies began a debate on which attunement would most help an author. Arabelle tried to focus on her work, though sometimes, instead of fabric, she imagined she was stitching Captain Parry again, and her stomach knotted. The captain showed no signs of fever this morning, and she prayed it would remain so, but this adventure was dragging her too far from the bounds of her comfort or expertise.

A loud crash and the rattle of breaking china sounded from the servant's corridor leading to the kitchens. A mishap for the maid, no doubt.

"Oh, poor girl!" Phoebe looked uncertain about how to respond.

"I'll see if she needs help," Arabelle said. After all, she wasn't a lady, so the maid need not be as humiliated in front of her.

She set her embroidery aside and stepped through the door that kept the servants' realm out of sight. Ruby bounded along at her heels. She let the door shut behind her, and it took her eyes a moment to adjust to the relative darkness.

A man stood in the dim corridor, crouched over the crumpled form of the maid. He'd raised his arm as though he'd knocked her down and was prepared to strike again.

Arabelle's blood ran hot. Whatever was happening, it was wrong.

"Stop!" Arabelle shouted, hoping the others heard through the thick door.

She stepped back to grab the door handle.

The man lunged and slapped her in the face so hard that black spots flashed in her vision. She covered her cheek and blinked at the tears of pain that ran down her face. She wanted to scream again, but she couldn't find her breath.

Her dragon growled and leaped forward, breathing flames at the intruder.

The man raised his arm to block the fire. His sleeve smoldered, but he smacked Ruby aside.

Arabelle gritted her teeth. No, no, no. This was like the Luddites all over again.

The faint ember smoldering on the man's linen sleeve called Arabelle. She fed it the anger and fear simmering in her belly.

The man's shirt combusted. He shrieked and dropped to the floor, thrashing about to put the flames out. Arabelle definitely heard French swearing.

The maid gaped at Arabelle in terror and scrambled away.

Arabelle gagged at the stink of singed hair. She covered her mouth and nose and staggered back. Had she hurt the poor maid or only frightened her further? Her hands trembled. What terrible power. This was not what she did best—not what she should be doing at all.

But it didn't matter what she thought. The others burst into the corridor. The man snarled and tried to rise, but Eliza's dragon joined Arabelle's in clamping down on the man's leg. He kicked them free, ignoring their renewed attack and pulling a pistol. The barrel turned on Arabelle.

Arabelle froze, her eyes fixed on the dark barrel, her limbs refusing to move. Fire was no help against bullets. This was not how she wanted to die. What had her life been? Gowns and lovely things for other people to go to parties while she watched on the side. She wanted...wanted to have danced again. Wanted to have read more novels. Wanted to not be alone.

The air turned frosty, and ice shot along the floor and up the man's body to grip him in place. Lord Westing strode down the corridor, his face frozen in fury.

Arabelle stepped out of the way of the pistol.

Lord Westing knelt by the frozen man and hit him in the face, cracking the ice from his mouth.

"Who sent you?" Lord Westing asked. He repeated the question in French.

The man said nothing, only smirked.

Lord Westing held his arm out, and his dragon hopped from his shoulder onto the intruder, digging icy talons into the man's exposed scalp.

Lord Westing clamped his fingers against the man's face. "You are already dangerously cold. Speak, or the ice will kill you."

Arabelle's heart beat hard. Was this what the dragon-linked were meant to do with their magic? Not that she thought Lord Westing was wrong to interrogate the man, but it turned her stomach. This power was not meant for her.

The man bit down hard on his own tongue and spit blood at Lord Westing.

Lord Westing recoiled, wiping his face clean. "Fanatic! You stay there until you die or we subdue all of your confederates." With a gesture from Lord Westing, the ice wrapped around the man's mouth, leaving only his nose and eyes free. Lord Westing looked at the ladies. "He won't be here alone."

"What does he want?" Phoebe asked, inching closer to her husband.

"He is French," Arabelle said. "I heard him swear."

Lord Westing muttered his own ungentlemanly words and drew Phoebe closer. Arabelle admired Phoebe for not fearing her husband's power.

"We stay together," Lord Westing said. "I'm certain this is related to the attack on Captain Parry—"

"Parry!" Eliza said.

She bolted for his room, and the others followed on her heels.

The captain was sleeping peacefully under the influence of laudanum.

"Safe!" Eliza breathed. She straightened, her eyes flashing. "And we will keep him that way. Shall we send our dragons to search for intruders? They can't speak to tell us what they find, but they have other ways."

Lord Westing nodded. His and Phoebe's dragons followed Eliza's. Arabelle looked to Ruby. Other than the Battle of the Tower, they'd had little experience with fighting. But her dragon seemed to sense what to do and flapped down the corridor after the others.

It wasn't long before a human shriek alerted them to the next invader. They hurried out, Lord Westing in the lead with Phoebe's hand firmly in his. Two men attempted to fight their way free from the dragons spewing various unpleasant concoctions at them.

"Shield your eyes," Lord Westing said in a low voice, then he nodded to Phoebe.

The intruders noticed them, but they weren't fast enough. Lord Westing created an orb of ice and sent it hurling through the air. Phoebe hummed something to herself, and the orb filled with blinding light. The men cursed and covered their eyes. The ice globe shattered, pounding the men with sharp shards.

"Mrs. Reynolds!" Lord Westing called. "Ring them in!"

He gestured to the candles burning along the walls.

Her heart skipped. She had never tried doing such a thing. She reached a hand for the candles. The flames sputtered. They were hungry, wanting to consume wick and wax and all beyond. Arabelle didn't dare tamper with such power. She would certainly set the house ablaze, and then they would all be in danger. The flames sputtered, dying.

She backed up, shaking her head.

Lord Westing growled and flung his hand out, sending ice crackling across the floor to hold the men in place.

The room was still dark. Much too dark. Something slithered and whispered in the shadows. The men in the center of the room went very still, watching in horror as darkness drew around them, speaking terrible things in a language that needed no translation.

"If you have harmed my wife, I will kill you very, very slowly," Lord Blackerby said from the entranceway.

"I'm here!" Amelia called.

She ran forward, and Lord Blackerby caught her in his arms, wrapping her in a tight embrace. The darkness in the room did not dissipate.

Lord Blackerby eased his hold on his wife and looked down at the men cowering in the center of the floor. "So, the French have come for our dragon-linked." He sneered at the men. "You needn't pretend you don't speak English. In an hour's time, I will have all of your secrets."

Chapter Thirteen

THE FRENCHMEN DIDN'T TAKE AS MUCH persuading as Farris had feared to reveal their plans to Blackerby. They even admitted to killing Croft, which erased any sympathy Farris might have felt for them. He disliked watching Blackerby's methods, though they mostly relied on intimidation. The shadows liked fear—hungered for it—digging into secrets and insecurities until people spoke just to bring the darkness into light and make the anguish stop. Blackerby never let the shadows have full rein, though Farris sensed it was a struggle for him.

It helped that Blackerby's dragon was venomous, and its bite inflicted another kind of torture.

"They were quick to speak," Farris said, as Blackerby locked the tied-up men in a room. "Do you think they told the whole truth?"

Some of the conversation had been in French, and Farris had only caught parts of it.

Blackerby sighed. "Enough of it. I think they told us because they believe we're too late."

"Too late?" Farris asked.

Blackerby motioned for Farris to follow him back to the drawing-room, where the others waited. Farris instantly looked to Arabelle. She looked tired and pale, but she was holding up well. From watching her, he knew that she did not like violence. Did not like using her powers. She belonged in a world of beautiful things. But she was stronger than she knew —strong enough to handle the other when it came her way.

Amelia rose to greet her husband, her eyes full of sympathy. She understood well how he disliked using the shadows, despite his air of nonchalance. Many of the dragon-linked did not enjoy using their powers in the ways they were called to in times of war. Westing had not hesitated to attack the intruders, but the tightness in his face showed what it had cost him.

"Well?" Westing asked.

"They are here for the Red Dragon," Blackerby said.

"They don't how to kill it, do they?" Phoebe asked.

"Thankfully, no," Blackerby said. "Shaw's knowledge died with him, as far as I can tell. No, they have a different strategy. They got word of the Battle of the Tower and how destructive a Great Dragon can be. They are hoping to provoke the Red Dragon to attack."

"Won't it just attack France in retaliation?" Arabelle asked.

Blackerby pursed his lips. "The White Dragon could not fly. He was too large and too old. The Red Dragon, we believe, is even older. She is the oldest dragon in the British Isles, if ancient records are to be believed."

"She must be enormous," Eliza said, her eyes distant. No

doubt remembering her own encounter with a Great Dragon. And that one was relatively young.

"Yes." Blackerby kept an arm around Amelia. "If she did stir out of her cavern, it would probably destroy the Welsh countryside. It would certainly disrupt our mining and ironworks, necessary to face Napoleon once again. And it would cause chaos and turn people against dragons."

"And she's supposed to be a fire dragon," Phoebe said softly, her eyes wide.

Farris glanced at Arabelle, who had gone a shade paler. Yes, if Arabelle and her dragon could so easily cause destruction, imagine what an ancient fire dragon could do if roused to a fury.

"And their plan is already in motion?" Westing asked.

"Yes," Blackerby said wearily. "They've smuggled in a small group of French dragon experts. They're already on their way to Dinas Emrys, where the dragon sleeps, hoping to goad her into attacking."

"We have to get there first!" Eliza said.

"My thoughts exactly," Blackerby said. "We can't take the roads. It's much too slow."

Eliza's eyes brightened. "You want to go by water?"

"Yes. But not around by sea. The waters are rough, and we'd still be behind them."

Eliza wrinkled her forehead. "You want…" Her confusion cleared. "You want to go up the river."

Blackerby nodded. "The Conwy is born in the mountains. If we can steer up it, we will cut days off our journey and perhaps beat the French to their destination. We can protect the Red Dragon. Mrs. Reynolds can speak to it before the French can."

Eliza closed her eyes and tilted her head as if listening. "I can feel the river. It is mighty—I could easily guide us up its waters." She looked at Blackerby. "But we can't leave Parry alone."

"Phoebe and I will stay," Westing said. "Our attunements are not as useful on this mission."

Blackerby nodded. "Excellent. Mrs. Parry, we may also need you to guide Mrs. Reynolds in contacting the dragon. And Farris and I will go as well, to protect the ladies."

"I'm coming, too," Amelia said.

Blackerby locked eyes with her, a silent domestic dispute occurring between them.

"I'm more likely to be of use up there than down here," Amelia said. "I don't have a dragon, but I have become a good shot with a pistol."

Blackerby sighed. "I cannot deny that. Very well. Is everyone satisfied with the arrangements?"

Farris scanned the room, but everyone nodded. None looked happy, but satisfied would have to do.

"Excellent," Blackerby said. "Because the tide is high. We must leave immediately."

Chapter Fourteen

ARABELLE HAD RARELY BEEN in a boat, and then just to traverse the Thames. She'd hardly even ventured outside of London's West End. Her shop on Bond Street was just a short walk from Sackville Street where her brother kept their family's jewelry shop. Where she'd grown up. Now, the wide waters of the Conwy rushed past the dock, making her lightheaded. This was too far from where she belonged.

What a ridiculous time to have such thoughts! She'd also never spoken to a dragon before. At least, not one that could speak back. Her pouch still held the useless yellow amethyst —a reminder of what happened when she stepped outside her abilities. But she had to try. Everyone was counting on her.

Lord Blackerby easily claimed a boat from a fisherman who was happy to "loan" it to them for the equivalent of a year's wages. Farris helped Arabelle into the rocking craft. Arabelle's nervousness made her hands cold, but Farris's touch—and his reassuring smile—warmed her.

"Never fear," Farris said. "It won't be worse than the ferries on the Thames. Better even, since Mrs. Parry is steering us. We'll reach Dinas Emrys in no time."

And then Arabelle had to save Britain from an annoyed dragon. The cold settled back over her, and she wrapped her arms around Ruby as the dragon nestled against her.

Lord Blackerby helped Eliza and Amelia into the boat. Once they were settled, he gave Eliza a nod. She pressed her lips together and studied the waters as if reading them. Then, she gestured, and the boat surged forward.

Arabelle gripped the side of the boat as the water flew by. Wind whipped her hair out of order, and water splashed as the boat cut through the lazy waves in the river. This was much faster than the ferries on the Thames. Her heartbeat raced, but she soon settled into the rhythm of the boat. It was like riding a horse. No, it was better. It was like flying—a feeling she had only dreamed of.

She glanced up to find Farris smiling at her, and she realized she was smiling as well.

Farris's knee pressed against hers, and she did not move away, glad to share the moment with someone.

The river valley sailed by, tiny farmhouses and ancient manors watching as they glided beneath their noses. But the French had a head start.

Despite Eliza's efforts and help from the incoming tide, their journey lasted over an hour. Plenty of time for Arabelle's hands to grow stiff with cold and her face to grow numb. She sheltered Ruby from the chilly wind that whipped over the little boat. Farris laid his cloak over her lap and her dragon. Its warmth soaked through her, but the wind quickly dissipated it. The cliffs rose up around them, making Arabelle feel very small indeed.

Her dragon nuzzled her clenched hand. She opened her palm, and the dragon coughed a little flame over it. She caught the fire and cradled it in her palms. It flushed warmth over her hands and sleeves, settling into her core to warm her. Next to her, Farris looked chilled. If only she could share the warmth with the others. If only she had worked to develop her skills. She had thought she would have time someday, not expecting someday to catch up with her.

By the time they reached the little village of Betws-y-Coed nestled in the mountains, the river grew too narrow and shallow to navigate, and Eliza looked ready to collapse. Farris took an oar to help the boat to the little dock, and Eliza sagged on her feet.

Arabelle let her flame go out.

Lord Blackerby and Amelia each took one of Eliza's arms and helped her ashore. Her dragon stumbled beside her, and she scooped it up to cradle it like an injured lamb.

Farris helped Arabelle from the boat and stayed near her side. She wished she could lean on him as Eliza leaned on Lord Blackerby and Amelia.

"I'll be fine," Eliza said blearily.

"Of course you will," Amelia said. "But you need rest now."

"I want to help," Eliza protested weakly. "They hurt Parry."

"And you have helped us avenge him neatly," Blackerby said. "We will see to the rest while you recover here in this inn."

Eliza pressed her lips together, but it was clear she knew she wasn't fighting Blackerby—she was fighting herself, and she could not win. She placed her hand on her growing belly, a reminder that she had other responsibilities to consider, and nodded.

Eliza turned to Arabelle. "I had hoped to help you when you spoke to the dragon, but I'll give you what advice I can. It will speak in your mind, and it should understand your spoken words. Most importantly, though, is you must embrace who you are. Embrace your element—your fire. That is what connects you to the dragon."

Arabelle nodded uncertainly and watched as Lord Blackerby helped Eliza into the inn. Embrace her fire. She did not really understand what Eliza meant. Arabelle pulled her hood up against the threatening rain. Her hands trembled, and she clasped them together.

"You can do this," Amelia said in a low voice.

Arabelle gave a start. She had almost missed the quiet woman standing next to her.

Arabelle shook her head. "I hope so, but...every time I've tried to use my magic, it's gone poorly. I've always thought... maybe I should not use it. I'm not worthy of it. If I could ever learn to be good at it, perhaps..."

But she did not try to be good at it, she admitted to herself. It had been less discouraging to put it off than to try and fail. And now she—everyone—was in a mess because of it.

Amelia studied her. "You think you're not worthy because you're not good at it?"

Arabelle flushed and shrugged one shoulder. "If I was worthy, wouldn't it come easily?"

Amelia made a little noise, almost a sniffle.

Arabelle looked down in alarm to find the woman tugging at a handkerchief. "I'm sorry! Did I say something wrong?"

"Not intentionally." Amelia drew a deep breath. "I have been hoping to become a mother, you see. So far, it hasn't happened for us. But—but I have to believe it's not because I am unworthy to be a mother."

Arabelle blanched. "No, of course not! I... I didn't mean it to sound that way."

"I know you didn't. I only told you because I think you need to know what I've learned. Our worthiness is not in what we accomplish, but in what we attempt."

"But..."

Amelia's idea flew against everything Arabelle had ever felt. Everything she had seen and heard in her father's jewelry shop. Everything had to be perfect, or it was not worth doing.

Yet what about Amelia's situation? Arabelle did not for a moment believe that Amelia was unworthy to be a mother because she had not yet conceived a child. That was nonsensical—something that couldn't be helped.

"I still believe it will happen for us someday, God willing," Amelia went on. "But in the meantime, I have found great satisfaction working with the children in the foundling hospital." A mischievous light entered her eyes. "I teach the girls art and writing, and they put even my melodramatic imagination to shame."

Lord Blackerby returned before Arabelle could think through everything Amelia had told her.

He looked them over. "I don't like leaving Mrs. Parry alone, but I understand it's best for Mrs. Reynolds not to travel alone with two men."

Arabelle flushed. "I am past the age where such a thing is a concern for me." There were advantages to not being a Society lady.

Amelia nodded. "Then I will stay with Eliza."

Lord Blackerby and Amelia whispered a few intimate words of farewell. Arabelle looked away, feeling like an intruder. Farris, she noted, was suddenly taking a great deal of interest in the village's ancient church.

After a moment, Amelia went to the inn, and Lord Blackerby straightened his waistcoat, polishing one of the brass buttons.

"Now then," he said. "We must move quickly and be on our guard. It's not just the French we have to concern ourselves with."

Arabelle gave him a confused look.

He raised an eyebrow. "We may also have an angry dragon to pacify."

Arabelle swallowed. An angry dragon for her to pacify. Whatever *someday* she had been waiting for, it had arrived like her most important client ringing the bell over her shop door.

Chapter Fifteen

IT WAS JUST AS WELL that the Great Dragons did not care about human fashions, because Arabelle's skirt was soaked in mud, and she huddled under her cloak with Ruby to fend off the spring chill.

Still, the mountains of Wales made her catch her breath at almost every twist of the trail. Spring runoff filled the streams and spilled over sharp edges as waterfalls, sometimes quick and dangerous, at others flowing down like the most translucent muslin. Delicate bluebells and dog violets livened the walk with their blue and purple flowers, and the blooms of gorse and broom added splashes of yellow and a sweet scent. All of the sights, shapes, and colors swirled in her mind into ideas for gowns, and her fingers itched her sketchbook. She had never imagined that her journey might bring inspiration, but she was certain *La Belle Assemblée* would rave about the new designs that Wales whispered to her.

Not only that, but she discovered that her stitching held

up just as well in the mountains of Wales as in the ballrooms of London. How many dressmakers could make that boast? She hiked her skirts up and marched on, keeping pace with the men.

Lord Blackerby led the way, his shadows spreading around him, no doubt seeking out the ancient secrets of the land. Farris walked a little slower, glancing back often to check on Arabelle. But she was proud to keep up and not need his assistance over any of the rougher parts of the trail or to step through the places where spring runoff had left the trail muddy.

Lord Blackerby rarely slowed, but at one point he did, his steps faltering and then stopping altogether.

"What is it?" Farris asked.

Lord Blackerby stared, his pupils going wide and dark. Unnaturally so.

A shiver of worry flew over Arabelle's skin. Something was wrong. Something lurked out there under the moldering stones with their thick covering of lichens.

"My lord!" Farris snapped.

Lord Blackerby gave a start and blinked, his eyes still too dark, but more natural looking. "The shadows like it here."

"There are ancient secrets out there," Farris said.

"Yes, for many lifetimes of man, shadows have lurked in these mountains and gathered whispers and memories like buttons and strings. In languages no man still speaks, except the shadows and keepers of secrets. And there is an ancient soul sleeping here…"

Lord Blackerby still didn't sound quite himself. Arabelle and Farris exchanged worried looks.

"Lord Blackerby," Farris said, emphasizing the name. Tying him back to himself. Even the great Lord Blackerby needed a stable hand on the reins at times. "What of the French?"

Lord Blackerby shook his head and drew a deep breath like a bloodhound after a scent. His shoulders relaxed. "Yes, I sense traces of their intent here. They are ahead, but we are gaining on them."

Farris nodded and hurried forward.

Lord Blackerby turned his still-too-dark gaze on Arabelle, and he smiled slightly. "You are keeping up admirably."

"Thank you," she said.

"You prove yourself strong, but remember, my dear, that there is also strength in reaching out to others."

She wrinkled her forehead.

Lord Blackerby stepped aside, and Arabelle saw Farris atop the boulder, reaching a hand back for Arabelle.

She could have scaled it herself. She might have scuffed herself up a bit, but she was capable of doing it. It felt good to be capable. Wouldn't her brother—her whole family, all those men in Society who looked down on her—be surprised to find she could do something so far outside her dressmaking shop?

But her brother wasn't here. Society wasn't here. Farris was, and he already believed her capable.

She reached out her hand and took his.

Chapter Sixteen

FARRIS WATCHED BLACKERBY WITH SUSPICION. Blackerby was tracking the French, diving deeper than he liked to with his shadows—deeper than might be safe in a place with a long and sometimes bloody history.

But Blackerby was quietly manipulating the situation to keep Farris and Arabelle together. Farris couldn't fathom why.

When Blackerby called for a brief rest for refreshment, Farris managed to pull him aside.

"What is your scheme?" Farris asked him.

"I thought it was obvious. We're hunting down the French and stopping their nefarious scheme."

"I mean with Mrs. Reynolds. You're plotting something else regarding her. Don't try to deny it."

"I don't deny it."

Farris's skin warmed. "If you're thinking of doing anything that puts her in more danger than she already is..."

Blackerby laughed. "Farris, you delightfully thick-skulled Scot, I'm plotting to allow you to charm her."

"To…what?"

Blackerby smirked. "This is why you need so many opportunities. Charm her."

Farris flushed this time. "I'm not certain she wants to be charmed. Especially not by me."

"You are blind. People usually are when it comes to their hearts. The rest of us have seen the way she looks at you."

"Does she?" Farris asked. "But she has a dragon. She could be a lady if she chose."

"But she did not choose it."

"She chose success in business instead. She wanted to be alone."

"I'm not sure anyone truly wishes to be alone," Blackerby said. "We might convince ourselves we do, but we have a need for company—for someone to hold to in the difficult times. In fact, that is why I've been trying to encourage you. You've been distracted of late—especially when Mrs. Reynolds is around."

"And the solution is to charm her into being around more?"

"To woo her, yes. Once you've secured her affections, you won't be so distracted."

Farris felt vaguely annoyed on Arabelle's behalf, but Blackerby always seemed to know what went on beneath the surface. Was it possible that Arabelle cared for him? Could Farris serve his country and a lady as well? She had been a dream for so long—not idealized, as he recognized her stubbornness as well as her beauty and cleverness—but it seemed impossible that a long-cherished dream could suddenly shift into something real, like shapes in the mist taking solid form. Yet here he was with Arabelle Reynolds in the mountains of Wales, and she had danced with him, and maybe he only needed to reach out to see if there was something substantial there after all.

When Arabelle joined them again, Farris smiled at her. She flushed and smiled back. Farris's chest warmed. Yes, maybe Blackerby did know what he spoke of.

They walked on, Farris keeping close to Arabelle. And she let him help her over the rough spots. It felt good to walk together.

Blackerby led the way, rarely pausing to determine his path.

"Not far now," Blackerby called back to them.

A bang echoed through the mountainside, and Blackerby stumbled. He took an unsteady step and collapsed.

"My lord!" Farris stepped forward.

"Stay back, fool, or they'll have your head!" Blackerby said. "They've only shot me in the leg."

He scootched his way back down the trail to duck behind one of the boulders and draw his own pistol. Farris drew as well. Arabelle looked pale and stood close to Farris, which did nothing to calm his rapid heartbeat.

Shadows formed a whirlpool on the ground around Blackerby.

The earl fastened his gaze on Farris and Arabelle. "Listen closely. We are close to Dinas Emrys. Clearly, the French are guarding the way. I will send a shadow to scout out a different path—you must follow it. Keep your head down and don't engage the French. I will keep them distracted. Your only job is to reach the dragon and speak to it. Make certain it knows our intentions are to help it. If you can, convince it that the French are the enemies and not us."

Arabelle still looked stunned, but Farris nodded his agreement and gently grasped her arm. She gave a start and looked between Blackerby and Farris, her eyes wide. Then, she took a shaky breath and nodded to Farris. A shadow swam along the ground, like a hound made of liquid, and they followed it off the trail and into the strange, rocky landscape of the high Welsh mountains.

Chapter Seventeen

ARABELLE STUMBLED ALONG, clinging to Farris's arm, trying to keep pace with the shadow darting ahead of them. Lord Blackerby was shot. He was shot, and the French guarded the way to Dinas Emrys. Her sharp breaths were as much from panic as from the race over the mountainside.

"Will he...will he be alright, do you think?" Arabelle gasped out.

A line of worry creased Farris's forehead, but then his face relaxed. "If anyone can survive those French b—...uh, trouble-makers, Lord Blackerby can. But we can't let him down. We have to do our part."

Arabelle nodded. The day had grown overcast, and the shadow's path was harder to follow. She didn't know if it had any intelligence of its own. Fire didn't, as far as she knew, but shadow was a different kind of element.

A gunshot echoed across the boulders.

"That sounded close," Arabelle hissed.

Farris nodded. He grabbed her hand to help her along,

and she didn't object. It felt natural, comfortable. Another gunshot rang out, and slivers of bark exploded off the oak tree next to them.

The French, just behind them. Did that mean Lord Blackerby had fallen? Maybe the French were too many even for him.

Farris pulled Arabelle behind a large outcrop of rock. He pointed up. Yes, they had reached the swell of Dinas Emrys. It was a steep rise—necessary to house the enormous dragon sleeping beneath it. Rocks and twisted oaks clung to its sides.

"We must be close to the dragon's cavern," Farris whispered. "The way inside."

"Where did the shadow go?" Arabelle scanned the ground, but there was no sign of it. Maybe it wasn't intelligent after all, and it had simply kept going for the dragon's lair without them. Maybe it was tied to Lord Blackerby, and he was...not able to control it anymore.

"There's a hillfort up there," Farris said. "If the French don't occupy it yet, we should try to claim it and find the cavern from there."

They picked their way a short distance up the steep slope, keeping their heads low, but Farris frowned and motioned for Arabelle to duck into a hiding spot behind another rocky outcrop.

He leaned in so that his breath tickled her ear. "I saw movement in the trees above. I think they've already occupied the hillfort."

Arabelle sighed and nodded. There would be no way for them to dislodge the French from their perch, then. The hillfort was built in that inaccessible place for a reason. The view stretched away forever, making it easy to detect enemies, and of course, there was the dragon—a friend to the

Welsh in olden times. And the French were now in a position to harass it.

"Can you sense the dragon?" Farris whispered. "Mrs. Parry said that she and her dragon could feel the Great Dragon when she drew close to it."

"I...I don't know." Arabelle swallowed, trying to steady her voice.

She closed her eyes. Nothing felt any different. Nothing spoke to her mind or her other senses. Ruby stayed close, sensitive to her agitation and unhappy with the cold. He gave no indication that he noticed anything out of the ordinary. Arabelle had been expecting to find the dragon's cavern—to see the dragon itself and not to seek out ephemeral traces of it. She'd expected to have more time.

Her throat tightened. "I'm not ready! I don't think I'm good enough. I don't think I ever will be."

Farris grabbed her hands. "Were you ready when you started your shop?"

"What?" Arabelle blinked, Farris's steady gaze anchoring her. "My shop? I was an excellent seamstress." The panic rose again in her chest, choking her.

"But were you a businesswoman?"

"My father... My family..." She took a shaky breath. "I knew a little, but mostly I knew how to sew."

Farris shifted his grip on her hands. "But you learned."

"Yes," Arabelle admitted quietly, remembering those early days when she struggled to manage appointments and bills and late, late nights working. "I learned. I had time to learn."

"You know more than you think," Farris said. "And now it's time to prove that by speaking to the dragon."

Arabelle drew a long breath. "I will try."

She squeezed her eyes shut. *Dragon, dragon, dragon. Good afternoon. Are you here?*

The heavy silence of the mountainside pressed against her ears, almost painful in its quiet. How she missed the noise of London!

Dragon? she thought into the stillness. *Can you hear me?*

Her cheeks warmed. What a fool she felt. And what if the dragon only spoke Welsh? Lord Blackerby might have been able to speak to it through her, but if the dragon didn't speak English, it wouldn't matter even if it could hear her.

What had Eliza told her? Focus on the connection to their shared element.

She concentrated harder, picturing flames crackling in a hearth. *Great dragon, I am also attuned to fire. I'm here to help you.*

Nothing. Still nothing in her head but her own scattered thoughts, flying every which way like spools of ribbon tipped over and unwinding across an empty floor. She was not the right person for this adventure. People were going to die because of it, if they hadn't already.

The wind carried voices to their hiding spot. Farris grasped her hand again, and she squeezed it back, desperately wishing she could sense anything of the Red Dragon.

She opened her eyes to study Ruby, but he was miserable with the cold and paid no heed to anything but burrowing into her cloak. How was she supposed to help anyone else when she could not even help herself and her little dragon? When the French were closing in on them, and they were out of time?

She met Farris's worried gaze and shook her head. He tilted his head close, his cheek warm next to hers.

"No fear, Mrs. Reynolds. You'll manage it. I know you will. And I will buy you time to do it."

"No!" Arabelle gasped.

But Farris was already gone. He darted out and down the steep side of the crag, releasing an avalanche of small stones to give away his position. The voices grew louder, shouting in alarm, and they followed Farris's retreat.

Arabelle caught Ruby in her arms and held him close, praying fervently that Farris escaped the French. She could not waste the opportunity he had given her, though.

She peered out. The coast appeared to be clear. She gathered Ruby close to her chest, trying to warm him, and snuck out of their hiding place in the direction she had last seen Lord Blackerby's shadow moving.

Arabelle had barely made it a few steps before someone shouted, "Arrête!"

She jumped and whirled to find a rough-looking Frenchman holding a musket on her. She gritted her teeth. Stupid women, useless outside of the shop and the sewing needle! Captured by the enemy. Kidnapped like a useless pawn. She looked into the man's eyes. No, there was no mercy there. She would not be held for ransom until a dashing hero came to her rescue. They might try to get information from her, but they were going to kill her.

Chapter Eighteen

WHAT A STUPID, meaningless way to die. Arabelle hadn't actually accomplished anything. She had finally run out of time.

Ruby launched himself at their captor. The man swung his musket up and fired.

Arabelle gasped. The Frenchman couldn't kill Ruby, but the dragon screeched when the musket ball struck home and knocked him out of the air.

Something flared deep in Arabelle's core, and she longed to smack the Frenchman. It reminded her of something she hadn't admitted when speaking to Farris. When she'd opened her shop, she'd burned with determination to succeed despite her shortcomings in business. She had her sewing skill, yes, but she'd also had her anger—anger at everyone who reminded her she wasn't good enough.

Ruby rose to his feet and spit fire at the Frenchman, but it fell short. The Frenchman laughed and reloaded his musket with expert speed.

An ember from Ruby's flame smoldered in the dried oak leaves underfoot. It was tiny glow, flickering like a fragile heartbeat, yet that was the thing about fire—it only needed a little spark to change everything.

Arabelle grimaced, gathered her anger and determination, and flicked her fingers. The flames roared up between her and the Frenchman.

He shouted in astonishment and stumbled back, dropping his gun. With a gesture from Arabelle, the flames encircled him. They licked over the gun, and the powder inside it exploded. Sparks flew onto the Frenchman's clothes, and he batted wildly to put them out.

Arabelle grabbed Ruby and fled, not daring to glance back at what she had done.

Instead, she looked toward Dinas Emrys. She had to *try* to finish her task. If only Farris… Her throat tightened, but she didn't let herself dwell on him. Not now. She prayed he had escaped.

She gathered her tattered hems and scrambled up Dinas Emrys, Ruby clutched in one arm. But the summit of the mountain was not her goal. The dragon was inside the mountain, not atop it like some ancient sage.

She stumbled forward, scanning the mountainside. There was no sign of Farris or Blackerby. She was alone, except perhaps the French who followed her, determined to kill the dragon-linked. It did not matter that she had not chosen to join Society. They hated her simply for what she was, not for any choices she had made.

Her gaze traveled upward and caught sight of something. At first, she mistook it for a figure standing on the ridge, and she flinched. But no, it wasn't a figure. It was a stone cross of the Celtic sort, lovingly carved and placed on that mountainside at some ancient date. That reminder that people had been in this place for so many years made her feel less alone. And why had they come? Because of the dragon. One that had once protected Britain. Perhaps that was almost two thousand years before, but what was two thousand years to an immortal guardian? Surely, the Red Dragon would not desert the nation now.

Her dragon made a clicking noise, suddenly on the alert. Had the French found her again?

She surveyed the landscape, hesitating a moment to decide where to go. There! Was that Blackerby's shadow lingering near an upturned stone beside the cross?

Arabelle hurried forward, winding her way through ancient trees, and the shadow shivered like a dog happy to see its master. Yes, the shadow had found something.

She followed it into the deeper shade beneath the stone and gasped. The cross wasn't just an ornament. It marked an ancient burial chamber built of huge slabs of stone. Arabelle ducked inside. The slabs of rock rose above her, sheltering her from enemy eyes. She wondered if it might lead to the Red Dragon's cavern, but if it once had, the way was now closed —just a wall of stone.

She sank against the ancient, chiseled wall, taking a moment to catch her breath. The chill seeped through her cloak, making her muscles stiff. She cradled Ruby, trying to warm him. He coughed a little flame onto some dried leaves blown into the burial chamber. Arabelle encouraged the flame to grow, hoping the smoke would not call attention to them. She would not let Ruby or herself freeze. She watched the flames dance.

Ruby burrowed under her cloak and tugged the pouch free that held his little hoard. Arabelle laid the gems out by the fire, and Ruby happily curled atop them. With his claw, he scratched aside the yellow amethyst and rested his chin on it.

Arabelle sighed. "Why do you dote on that one so? It's worthless, you know."

She curled her knees up to her chest and crossed her arms on them to rest her head. Worthless. It was her brother's word, but it never seemed to stop ringing in her ears. A stubborn piece of lint she could never pick off. And like a rogue ball of lint, it picked up more dust and dirt as it tumbled through the years. Through London Society. *She may have a dragon, but she smells of the shops... Unnatural... Dangerous... Can't she do more than watch as Westminster burns?... Stop! It will absorb any magic we use against it. Do not give it fire...*

Ruby nuzzled her knee and pushed the yellow amethyst over to her. She grimaced and picked the stone up, holding it so the light played off it. Her father had told her that some people created false diamonds by heating sapphires. That heat sometimes improved the color of stones. And her brother's amethyst had poor color. She thought she could make it better for him. She never should have interfered with his project.

The light winked off the amethyst, showing its clear yellow. She sighed. Despite the way everyone had reacted, she still thought the stone looked better now. Of course, she understood that a yellow stone was not useful in a collection of jewels that were supposed to be purple. Though, her eye for color told her the two could look well together. If anything, had it been her design, she would have reordered it around the yellow stone.

Ruby sprung to Arabelle's shoulder, leaving his hoard to glitter in the firelight. She picked up a few of the purple stones and rearranged them around the yellow one. A smile crept over her lips. It was a lovely design—her eye for fashion reassured her that she was correct about that.

She scooped the other stones back into the pouch and held the amethyst up again.

"It's not worthless. He was just using it wrong."

Could that be true of her magic as well? Eliza had said it was a part of her. Arabelle had come to think of it as a dangerous part—too hot to touch lest she be burned. She watched the flames crackling, sensed their hunger—but it wasn't a greedy hunger at the moment. It was excitement. The thrill of living, even knowing that life would someday burn out. Giving energy and beauty and even life to those in its circle. Wasn't that what Arabelle always wanted to do with her designs? If only she could do it with her magic, too.

She leaned against the cold stone wall and closed her eyes. Ruby curled up in her lap, and she focused on the warmth between them. The warmth multiplied, spreading through her core, out her limbs, and into the stone at her back.

She pictured Farris out there, cleverly dodging the French—she hoped. She wished she could send some of the warmth to him as well. She imagined, at least, that she could do so, focusing on warmth traveling through the earth to reach him until she swore she saw him—indeed, hiding from the French and worrying about her. She stretched a hand out to the picture in her mind, willing the warmth to him like a summer breeze. He furrowed his brow and looked around in confusion.

It was a pleasant daydream. What of Lord Blackerby? If he was alive, he would be cold. She let her mind search him out as well. She imagined she saw him propped against a rock— alive and angry, though blood soaked down into his boot and he shivered while his shadows circled in frustrated waiting. She willed warmth to him as well, imagining the rock behind him as a heated hearthstone. The lines of pain in his face relaxed, and his eyes lit with excitement.

"Mrs. Reynolds, what have you done?" he asked himself, then chuckled.

Now her imagination was getting quite out of hand. The cavern in which she hid even felt more pleasant—the rocks all around heating as though warmed by some inner, living fire. And an image swam into her mind of a monstrous dragon sleeping deep in the earth, rock growing around the creature in its slumber. Flames flickered in and out around it, and it rested uneasily, its mighty muscles tensed and its huge wings drawn tight over its shimmering red scales.

Who are these people who come to my mountain?

Chapter Nineteen

ARABELLE STARTED and opened her eyes. The voice had seemed so real. She must have slipped into a dream.

Who are you who brings flame to my mountain? It has had been many years since anyone shared their warmth with me.

The voice echoing in her head sounded old. So old and creaky that she could not determine if it was male or female. Almost as ancient as the stones of the mountain and the winds that whistled over the peaks. But alive in her mind.

Ruby climbed out of her lap and scurried around the chamber, sniffing at corners as if hunting. The ground rumbled, rattling small stones scattered around the chamber. Was the dragon's voice more than a figment of her imagination?

"I am Arabelle Reynolds," she said, feeling absolutely foolish talking aloud to a voice in her mind. "I am attuned to fire. Is this the Great Red Dragon of Wales who does me the honor of speaking to me?"

There was a long silence. She must have imagined it after

all. She didn't even know if Farris and Lord Blackerby were alive, or how long until her little fire ran out of fuel and the cold—or the French—claimed her.

A sound like a chuckle rolled through her mind. *Is that what they call me? What a burden of a name.*

Arabelle gave a start and looked around, but of course, it was still only her and Ruby in the chamber. "Uh, what do you prefer to be called?"

Many centuries ago, a human gave me the name Ember.

Arabelle had the distinct sense that the dragon was speaking in ideas more than words. They did not speak the same language—not strictly—but they shared something that allowed their hearts and minds to understand each other.

It is an appropriate name. I'm not certain there is much fire left in me anymore.

"Oh. I'm afraid I have let my fire go dim, too. It can be a frightening thing, the destructive power of fire… I don't think I quite knew what to do with it."

What a silly thing to say to a creature that lived and breathed fire magic.

Anything can be frightening if allowed to rage out of control. Yet when properly harnessed, it is a thing of beauty and a force for change. It makes raw foods good for humans to eat, dull hunks of metal into useful tools, and impure things bright and clean once again. Fire flows through the veins of the earth, bringing all the elements into one.

"Oh! I never thought of…of anything beyond making tea and lighting candles, I suppose."

Perhaps it is time to begin. I imagine some great need brought you to my mountain? The land is ill at ease.

"Yes." Arabelle roused from her wonder to remember what had brought her there. "We have felt the earth shifting.

Felt your...discomfort, perhaps? We wanted you to know we are allies. Not like some others who have hunted dragons. Who are hunting dragons now."

Hmm. The ravens whisper in my dreams of enemies. Of my mate in a terrible battle. I have rested less easily, uncertain what I might do. I would not like to unleash fire on my own lands.

"No. At least, I hope that won't be necessary. We would value your help, though. Even your wisdom."

I cannot fight as once I might have. The centuries weigh too heavily on me. My body will no longer fit through any openings of my cavern, so I have become a prisoner in my chamber, unless the need is so urgent that I should inflict great damage on my mountain and the shepherds and others who travel near it. I could summon younger dragons to your aid, but there are not many near. None that could arrive soon except your own and a shadow dragon. After so many centuries, my abilities are limited.

Arabelle chuckled to herself. Had she really ever thought three and a half decades was old? "I believe that even a small show of your support for us would discourage the French invaders."

The dragon was quiet for a time, but Arabelle felt her presence like a warm breeze brushing over her mind, gleaning her thoughts.

Then Ember returned her chuckle. *I see. Yes. It has been rather dull these last few centuries. Stirring up a little trouble will give me something pleasant to dream of when I return to slumber. I believe I can also lend more sparks to your tricks.*

Arabelle took a deep breath. "I am ready then. Where do we find the French?"

Chapter Twenty

ARABELLE EXITED THE CHAMBER, Ruby on her shoulder. The chill wind blowing through the oaks stole her breath. But there was a warmth inside her, and she knew that this time it would not fail her. She hiked toward the hilltop fortress where the French had taken command.

She held out her hand, and Ruby ignited a spark for her to cradle in her palm. The heat of it prickled over her skin, warming her cheeks. She walked alone, but not entirely cut off. The Red Dragon's presence rested against her awareness. And somewhere, she believed, Lord Blackerby and Farris were doing their parts.

She strode into view of the French, and before they could do more than come to attention, she threw the fire at them. It grew into a tremendous fireball, slamming into the ground in front of the hillfort. No need to damage the ancient ruins— she just had to drive the French back from the walls.

A few fired guns at her, but she wove between the ancient

oaks of the mountain. At that distance, the shots fell short. Ruby coughed a second burst of flame, which she caught and caused to grow up into a large column of fire in her hands. It nearly tipped out of her command, but she steadied herself with a deep breath. Keep it under control. She only had to focus on her part.

The ground trembled, eliciting a shout from the hillfort.

"Mrs. Reynolds!" Lord Blackerby called from somewhere behind her.

She couldn't spare a glance back. Lord Blackerby had brought her to Wales because she was the only one who could do this, and now he was going to have to trust his decision—trust her. She was glad he was well, though. Alive, anyway. His voice sounded pained. He did not come closer, but his dragon swooped up beside her. Venomous bite, she recalled.

The ground shook again. This time, a few loose rocks tumbled down the mountainside, creating a terrible clatter on their way and landing at the bottom with a shattering explosion of dust and rock shards.

Arabelle kept her balance. Some of the men in the hillfort did not appear so fortunate. They tried to stand, and the ground rumbled again. Rocks pushed up around the ruins of the fort, some tumbling down the steep mountainside. The French scrambled free of the ancient fortress. Arabelle cast her fire once again to encourage them to go the other way—toward the steepest side of the mountain.

The ground at the summit heaved up, lifting, lifting, lifting. A stone rose from the center. A red tint fell over it—over everything, it seemed. Because it wasn't rock at all. It was the top of the dragon's head. The stone above it had formed into something like a helmet, great shafts of rock rising like horns. Its scales shimmered a fiery red like the heart of a hearth. The curve of its skull was surprisingly graceful, its dark eyes huge as it surveyed the tiny French interlopers. It bared teeth that were sharp and ivory colored even after so long sleeping.

The French spies recoiled in horror, mute with terror. They could not have imagined what a behemoth they were awakening.

"The Red Dragon of Wales has a message for Napoleon!" Arabelle shouted. "Tell him Britain is for its dragons, and its dragons are for Britain."

Not exactly my words, but well enough. Now for the rest of the message.

Ember extended her jaw and exhaled a burst of flame into the air. Even at that distance, Arabelle felt the heat.

The spies did, too. One of them actually attempted to approach the dragon, and Arabelle gave him credit for either bravery or stupidity—how often those lines crossed.

Ember roared, a sound that shook the ground and the leaves of the oaks and made the air shimmer with its intensity, like waves of heat rising from a fire.

The French yowled and stumbled and fell into disorderly retreat, half sliding and half falling down the steep side of the mountain, bouncing their way around boulders.

Ember blasted another column of flame over their heads in farewell.

The Red Dragon turned back to Arabelle and surveyed her with those massive, dark eyes. Then she yawned.

I believe they understood the message. I find Wales much too chilly in the spring, however, especially at my age, so I will return to my slumbers now.

"Thank you!" Arabelle called.

She swore the mighty creature winked at her. And then it

pulled its head back into the ground, allowing an avalanche of loose rocks to tumble down and fill in the hole above its stony helmet once again.

Arabelle's heart pounded in exhilaration. That had been better even than designing the most stunning gown. *Ackermann's* and *La Belle Assemblée* could never offer her such a thrill.

"I knew you would do it!" Farris called.

He limped down from what must have been a very precarious hiding place near the hillfort. He hurried forward and clasped Arabelle's hands. She laughed in pure happiness and relief at seeing him there and threw her arms around him. He hesitated only a moment before engulfing her in his strong embrace and cradling her head against his broad chest.

He pulled back to look at her, and his face grew more serious. "Where is Lord Blackerby?"

"I heard him." Arabelle turned to scan the landscape. "His dragon was here."

"There!"

Farris rushed toward a form Arabelle would have taken for just another shadow. But no, Lord Blackerby had drawn the shadows about him like a cloak, hiding his presence. As she came closer, Arabelle saw why. Blood covered his leg, and he looked on the verge of passing out.

Blackerby fixed still-sharp eyes on her. "I don't suppose your new friend will offer us transportation back down the mountain?"

"She cannot leave the mountain any longer," Arabelle said regretfully. Lord Blackerby would have a difficult time making it back down on that leg.

"I think the Red Dragon did not forget us," Farris said, pointing.

Eliza strode up the mountain, Amelia close behind her. A man and a boy, both with dragons, accompanied them. The Red Dragon had summoned the nearby dragons after all.

"In that case," Lord Blackerby said, letting his eyes sag shut, "I think it is time I took a rest."

Chapter Twenty-One

ARABELLE FLIPPED through the pages of *La Belle Assemblée*, still struggling to believe that those were her designs receiving its praise. The writers liked her military details, noting however that they were rather obvious, and reserved their greatest accolades for the floral designs she had begun working on as soon as she returned from Wales. Her brother had even bothered to send a message from the family jewelry shop to congratulate her on her success. She had returned a quick note to him, but she found she neither craved nor despised his praise any longer.

The Arabelle before Wales would have fretted still, trying to scratch together even more reassurance of her success, perhaps chasing another recognition, but Arabelle now was able to survey the happy clients in her shop and the half-constructed gowns that would certainly shine at the theater or in the ballroom, and hum in contentment. She was excited for *La Belle Assemblée* and the rest of Society to see how she would integrate fire magic into fashion. She was already learning to burn designs into delicate leathers, and she wanted to try other materials as well. *La Belle Assemblée* might be slow to praise something so innovative, but Arabelle was pleased with her designs so far, and her clients clamored for more of her decorated gloves and reticules.

She spotted Farris's red hair through the window. Her face broke into a grin. He smiled back when he saw her and hurried into the shop, drawing curious gazes from several young ladies examining a bolt of sprigged muslin.

Normally, he waited until after business hours to visit or lingered on the threshold so as not to disturb this female sanctuary, but today he rushed to embrace Arabelle.

"It's over!" he boomed.

She returned his embrace. "Over? What—"

"Napoleon! There was a battle this morning near a little Belgian town called Waterloo. The White Dragon was able to send some foul weather to slow their cannon, and we delivered a stunning defeat."

"Napoleon is dead?" Arabelle asked, a little dazed.

"No, captured again. But he had surrendered and abdicated his throne. The fighting is over."

The girls in the shop cheered and broke into circles of giddy chatter.

Arabelle sank into Farris's arms. "I'm so glad! But you're certain? Did you just hear?"

"Yes. The Duke of Wellington managed to send a message carried by his dragon."

"Lord Blackerby must be relieved."

Farris chuckled. "He's annoyed that he couldn't be there. His leg is mostly mended, but he's not ready for battle quite yet. His wife would never allow it."

Arabelle laughed at that cozy domestic image. "I imagine

not. Well, it sounds like we have the chance to celebrate before everyone else."

"Right now?" Farris asked. "I've no complaints, but your shop's even more busy since the article."

Arabelle smiled at her assistant. "Maria can manage things for a while. She's very competent, and I don't think we ought to put things off that we could do right now. We deserve a little time to celebrate."

Maria beamed and nodded.

Arabelle grinned at Farris. "There, you see. And I hope you have finished *Mansfield Park* as you promised so we can discuss it."

He wrinkled his nose. "I did. I thought Edmund was a fool." His eyes brightened. "But the story as a whole put me in mind of something I've been wanting to ask you, especially now that the trouble with Napoleon is over."

He smiled shyly and offered an arm to Arabelle. She gladly took it. Ruby jumped to her shoulder, and they strolled out into the bright light of a sunny London afternoon. She had a sense of the question Farris planned to ask, and it felt like a perfect day to say yes.

Author's Note

I hope you have enjoyed this return to the world of the Dragons of Mayfair. As with the other books in the series, I have tried to keep the general facts and dates in alignment with history, including Napoleon's escape from exile and defeat at Waterloo in 1815, and the volcanic eruption whose lingering ash would cause 1816 to be "the year without a summer," though of course adding dragons into the mix.

Wales really is subject to earthquakes from time to time. It also has several extinct volcanos, though none of them have been active during human history. Dinas Emrys is one of these ancient volcanic outcrops. It's the site where the legendary Red Dragon of Wales rested, and where King Arthur's enemy Vortigern learned from Merlin or Ambrosius Aurelianus aka Emrys (depending on the story) that the Red Dragon of Wales would conquer the White Dragon of England (which I suppose makes the relationship I have invented between those dragons an enemies-to-lovers romance). The ruins of a hillfort sit atop the rise, and the oldest portions of them date to the Roman and post-Roman era, which is the right timing for a connection to the historical figures behind Ambrosius, Vortigern, and Arthur. There is even a pool in the ruins, which coincides with the legend of the Red Dragon, though if she is there, she's sleeping very soundly these days.

Mansfield Park was Jane Austen's third published book, printed in 1814. During her lifetime, the books were published anonymously since making money was a shocking necessity for the upper classes—and especially for women. Jane Austen had two brothers in the navy, which influenced the naval characters in her books and her references to the West Indies. *Mansfield Park* dealt with even heavier social issues than *Sense and Sensibility* or *Pride and Prejudice* (and under their sparkling characters and happy endings, they all touch on distressing social problems of the time), including a reference to the debate over slavery and its use in West Indies sugar plantations. Jane Austen didn't need magic to be a great observer of people and an insightful writer, but if she did have a dragon in this alternate world, I think she would have been attuned to light.

Changing the color of gems with heat is common today, and jewelers were experimenting with it in in Regency era and even before. It takes a great deal of control to apply the right amount of heat for the right amount of time without cracking the stone, so for Arabelle to have done so successfully would mean that she was very skilled at controlling her ability. The craftsmanship involved was uncommon, though, and she wouldn't have realized the extent of her success, which happens too often among people brave enough to blaze new trails.

Also by E.B. Wheeler

British Fiction:

Born to Treason

The Royalist's Daughter

The Haunting of Springett Hall

Wishwood (Westwood Gothic)

Moon Hollow (Westwood Gothic)

A Proper Dragon (Dragons of Mayfair 1)

An Elusive Dragon (Dragons of Mayfair 2)

A Subtle Dragon (Dragons of Mayfair 3)

Cruel Magic (Iron & Thorns 1)

Wild Magic (Iron & Thorns 2)

Fierce Magic (Iron & Thorns 3)

A Haunted Masquerade (A Haunted Season)

Utah Fiction:

No Peace with the Dawn (with Jeffery Bateman)

Letters from the Homefront (Utah at War)

Balm for the Heart (Utah at War)

Bootleggers and Basil (in *The Pathways to the Heart*)

Blood in a Dry Town (Tenny Mateo Mystery 1)

A Company of Bones (Tenny Mateo Mystery 2)

Nonfiction:

Utah Women: Pioneers, Poets & Politicians

Mysteries of the Old West

Mysteries of the Middle Ages

Mysteries of the Modern World

Juvenile Fiction:

The Bone Map

Alejandra the Axolotl and the Big Mess

Acknowledgments

Thank you to my critique group The Writers' Cache and to my beta readers, Dan, Karen, Lauren, and Zoey for their feedback and encouragement. And as always, I couldn't do this without the understanding, patience, and support of my family and especially my husband.

About the Author

E.B. Wheeler attended BYU, majoring in history with an English minor, and earned graduate degrees in history and landscape architecture from Utah State University. She's the author of over a dozen books, including Whitney Award finalists *Born to Treason, A Proper Dragon, A Haunted Masquerade,* and *Fierce Magic,* and Whitney Award winner *Cruel Magic,* as well as several short stories, magazine articles, and scripts for educational programs. The League of Utah Writers named her the Writer of the Year in 2016. In addition to writing, she sometimes consults about historic preservation and teaches history.

www.ingramcontent.com/pod-product-compliance
Lightning Source LLC
Chambersburg PA
CBHW051258170626
46809CB00004B/1712